Odile

Raymond Queneau

INTRODUCTION BY THE TRANSLATOR
CAROL SANDERS

Dalkey Archive Press

Originally published by Editions Gallimard, 1937
Copyright ©1937 Editions Gallimard
This translation and Introduction copyright © 1988 Carol Sanders
English language copyright © 1988 The Dalkey Archive Press

Library of Congress Cataloging-in-Publication Data:

Queneau, Raymond, 1903-1976.
        [*Odile*. English]
        Odile / Raymond Queneau: translated by Carol Sanders.
        Translation of: *Odile*.
PQ2633.U430413   1988   843'.912—dc19   88-25051
ISBN: 1-56478-209-3

Partially funded by grants from the National Endowment for the Arts, a federal
agency, and the Illinois Arts Council, a state agency.

Dalkey Archive Press
Illinois State University
Campus Box 4241
Normal, IL 61790-4241

visit our website: www.dalkeyarchive.com

Introduction

Odile, first published in French in 1937, is a gentle story about the growth of love and of self-awareness, set against the turbulent background of literary and political life in Paris between the wars. Readers familiar with this period will recognize aspects of the events and characters, although in this semi-autobiographical novel, memories are selected, conflated, transformed. Indeed, the difficulty of conjuring up the past, and the distance between the present narrator and his past self, are themes that run throughout the novel. The lyrical sobriety of much of the narrative, found also in another early novel, *A Hard Winter* (1939), contrasts with the rollicking use of wordplay and slang that characterizes some of Queneau's better known novels such as *Zazie in the Metro* (1959). But in *Odile* there is no lack of lively dialogue, a sprinkling of puns, a mischievous mix of high and low styles, and references—often delightfully ironical—to contemporary colloquialisms and the mores they reveal. And of course there is vehement, if humorous, satire of the literary and political factions involved.

It is no secret that there are many points of similarity between Anglares's group in the novel and the Surrealists under André Breton, including their flirtation with Communism. Critics have tended to play down Queneau's involvement with the Surrealist group. In literary terms, however, there is much that he shares with them, including the use of verbal experimentation and wordplay to rejuvenate language and to liberate the unconscious. Also, strongly reflected in Queneau's novels are his interest in dream (as in *The Blue Flowers,* 1975), in coincidence and in certain aspects

i

of occult thought. More important, perhaps in the context of *Odile,* is the fact that the love of one woman as a redeeming and sublime force leading to self-knowledge was a constant theme for the Surrealists, as, for example, in the poetry of Paul Eluard.

There are also, however, major questions on which Queneau diverged from the Surrealists, such as automatic writing and inspiration, about which a debate takes place in the pages of *Odile.* Nor was the Surrealists' homage to irrationality likely to have been to the taste of this predominantly rational skeptic, a point well made by Allen Thiher in a recent study (*Raymond Queneau,* Twayne, 1985). Queneau did not observe some of the self-imposed restrictions of the Surrealists. He ranges across art forms and genres, drawing on the whole French literary inheritance. Where Breton condemns the novel, Queneau revitalizes it in a way that anticipates the French New Novel. He has a scholarly interest in a number of disciplines, from German philosophy to linguistics and . . . mathematics. All in all, Queneau is too much of an eclectic thinker, too much of a hater of systems and *isms,* of mystification and personality cults, to have lasted in the Surrealist movement—or in the Communist Party.

To put all of this in a different perspective, that of chronology, Queneau left his native Le Havre in 1920 to study philosophy in Paris. In 1924 he was introduced to the Surrealist group by Pierre Naville, and was an early contributor to the review *La Révolution Surréaliste.* After Breton, Aragon, Eluard and Péret had made a formal break with Dadaism in 1922, they and others had been engaged on a far-reaching series of experiments, involving prognostications, hypnosis, sleep and automatic writing. As Maurice Nadeau wrote, "The movement was envisaged by its founders not as a new artistic school, but as a means of knowledge." They met at Breton's house, or in cafés (moving from Le Grillon in the Passage de l'Opéra to the Cyrano in the Place Blanche), and took long walks through the streets of Paris, as described in Aragon's *Le Paysan de Paris*. Their activities culminated in 1924 in the first Surrealist Manifesto, and in the setting up of a "Bureau for Surrealist Research." An intense debate began about association with the *Clarté* review group and about possible membership in the Communist Party. Evidence of Queneau's involvement around this time is found in a photo taken in the Bureau, and his name appearing on various notices and tracts. The 1925 declaration, *La Révolution d'abord et toujours!* (Revolution Now and Forever!), signed by Queneau as an "independent," was prompted by the outbreak of the Moroccan war, and states categorically the belief that any revolution must be first and foremost a social one.

Queneau's involvement was in fact interrupted from October 1925 to February 1927 by military service, mostly in North Africa, which is the setting for the opening pages of *Odile*. After his return to Paris, Queneau got married (to the sister of Breton's first wife). For a while he again participated in Surrealist activity, speaking on the question of individual versus communal action at a decisive meeting called in March 1929 in the Rue du Château to discuss the exiling of Trotsky from the USSR. However, Queneau broke with Breton later that year, although the latter in his *Entretiens* speaks favorably of Queneau and regrets his departure from the group.

To continue the story a little, Breton who had joined the Communist Party in 1927, did not remain a member for long. Aragon (charged by Breton with being too literary and insufficiently politicized!) gave up Surrealism for Marxism and Realism, while Surrealism itself continued to grow internationally, mainly as a literary and artistic movement. Queneau pursued his quiet resistance to totalitarianism and all forms of regimented thought, for example contributing to Boris Souvarine's *Critique Sociale* in the 1930s.

Like Travy in *Odile*, Queneau visited Greece in summer

1932; he published his first novel, *The Bark-Tree,* in the same year, *Odile* in 1937 and many other novels and poems besides in years to come. But these are other stories and other novels, which it is hoped the reader may be tempted to follow up after reading *Odile.*

Acknowledgments: I am especially grateful to Louise Maurer for her collaboration, and to the Australian National University for providing the funds to make her assistance possible. I am much indebted to Peter Figueroa for his many helpful comments. Thanks also goes to all the others who showed an interest in the translation or made suggestions, including P. Cossey, Paul Figueroa, J. Grieve, R. Hillman, R. Ireland, G. Moliterno and L. Nichols.

Carol Sanders

this translation is for Barbara Wright and Claude Rameil,
two indefatigable Queneauphiles

ODILE

As this story begins, I am on the road between Bou Jeloud and Bab Fetouh which skirts the walls of the town. It's been raining. The last of the clouds are reflected in puddles of water. The slime oozes under my boots. I am dirty and shabby, a soldier returning from four months with an expeditionary force. Ahead of me motionless, gazing at land and sky, is an Arab. He has the noble air of a poet, or a philosopher. That's how this story begins. There is, however, a prologue, and even though I can't remember my childhood, my memory being as if ravaged by some disaster, there nevertheless remains a series of images from the time before my birth. Later on, people said that I couldn't have been born like that, at twenty-one years of age, with my feet in the mud, surrounded by puddles, and, up above, the last stragglers of a beaten battalion of clouds; yet that is how it is: of my first twenty years, only ruins are left in a memory devastated by unhappiness.

As this story begins, I had been a soldier for nearly a year, and had just spent the past four months in the Rif. I had seen men killed and villages burned down. I was one of the invaders, yet I loathed the arrogance of my filthy, ignorant companions, most of them really good guys and all capable no doubt of making really good butchers. I was just as filthy but not such a good guy. My sympathies lay elsewhere. Still, I had to do what I was told, and even if I myself had not fired on the Shleuhs, I had nevertheless taken part in the expeditionary force that was zealously carrying on the work of Charles Martel and the Cid Campeador.

We began by coming to a halt at a stronghold made of stones, under which the highest ranking and smartest of us grabbed a place. The rest, including me, catnapped under a tent called a marabout and stood guard for three hours a night. It never stopped raining, like in a proper European war, a great war. We lived in rust, kept barely alive by rotting food. That went on for nearly a month; then they took us up onto a small plateau, flattened by the wind, that the military had declared to be a safe area. You could in fact watch the comings up and goings down of convoys of mules; battalions of legionnaires, guerrillas, and other strange sights. You had to cross a ford to fetch your grub. That way your feet got a wash. All this is only of the slightest interest, but after all, it's the prologue of this tale, and I know what I'm doing; I don't tell my stories just any old way. So then, like that our feet got a wash.

When our superiors decided that our feet were clean enough, we struck camp and went higher into the mountains to relieve God-only-knows-now-which battalion that was about to be sent into action. We were scattered in very small fortified posts; mine surrounded the tomb of an Islamic saint. There was a spring at the center of the battalion, and just outside the Berber village, a trader sold wine and canned food. We were close to the border with Spanish Morocco, and the villages ahead of us were still in rebellion. They were being bombarded in every imaginable way. Further off, you could see a large village that was like a kind of Mecca to me. I hoped that we would reach it; my love of travel, you understand.

Apart from the tomb, there was a cannon and an expert who made it go bang. As soon as he saw a couple of Arabs down below, he took aim and missed. He also kept himself amused by painting watercolors on aloe leaves, and he used to sing a song which went something like "he knew how to lie to calm our silly fears." Nice to see a maiden happy in her work. We kept watch over the tomb of the saint and built low walls with stones that were guarded by scorpions and snakes, but the only thing that interested me was the township where we did not go.

The war drew to a close. There was an offensive. The rebel villages caught fire one after the other, lighting up the onward march of victory like the little flags on the local café back home. At dawn green rockets soared into the sky: the expert was aiming his cannon at ruins that had already felt the hand of civilization. During the night the fires died down. We never went to Taberrant, the town in the mountains, but they made us march around to get some blisters. We cut right through the middle of fields of wheat; there were meadows covered in blue flowers that are called something in literature. The conquered natives were selling raisins and the sergeants bought the favors of their daughters for the price of a crust of bread, or so they boasted. We moved camp nearly every day; the only memory I have left is of the saint's tomb and the name of the town. Then our company went down into a basin where there was a supply base. Our main function was still to keep guard; we also carted around sacks of grain and blankets bundled up with wire. Because of my education, I was given the job of filing coupons for rice and lentils; at night I felt like a shepherd. The hours of guard duty were long and empty, and while I watched the moon wax, the rams fought in the pen, their skulls resounding through the silence. Other features of interest were a church made of wooden planks that was blown apart in a storm, and souks where you could drink Pernod and which got demolished as well. There was a market once or twice a week by the river. I especially liked the snake charmer; he used to pick out a snake, bite off its head, skin it and hand around the bits of skin. There's nothing like travel to broaden the mind.

I don't know how long I stayed in that particular place; my poor memory is not a chronometer, nor a movie camera, nor a phonograph, nor any other sort of finely tuned machine. It's more like nature, with holes, empty spaces, hidden nooks and crannies, with rivers that trickle away, so that you can never dip your foot in the same water twice, and with patches of light and darkness. Out in the hot sun there was a prison, a barbed-wire cage in which prisoners from the Rif dragged themselves about in chains like convicts, staggering around attached to telegraph poles. One screamed out in the night and died: they said he was beaten to death. This too was like a proper war, a little Great War. Some time after, I was posted to Fez to act as secretary to the commander who commanded operational headquarters for that area. Despite my naive look, I had landed myself what military slang calls a cushy job. Two other chosen ones and I got into the truck that was to take us to the camp at Prokos along a dusty, broken-up road.

I learned to type. It really was a cushy job. I could only explain it properly by using a string of technical terms. Until I was demobilized, I never had to do guard duty again, never had to parade for inspection, never had to do drill or to lay my hands on a gun. We were simply clerical staff, and the one time that at the whim of an officer we had to perform as soldiers at a big ceremony we made such a lamentable showing that they stuck us behind a shed to watch the spahis ride past and the Foreign Legion present arms in model fashion. What's more, we were allowed into town every evening, all night. G. never went further than the Jewish quarter. I explored the Arab town with S. The only thing that G. liked about the Arabs was that they were victims of French colonial oppression, because he was a communist. He felt no sympathy for their civilization, scorning it as feudal. It was only the thought of imperialism as the last stage of capitalism that stopped him from calling the

Arabs by the charming little names generally used by colonial masters. He was some guy, was G. He could knock back a bottle of booze (as he referred to that red liquid whose density frequently resembles that of water) faster than anyone. G. wanted to be thought of as a member of the Parisian proletariat. He told funny stories (d'you know this one?) and claimed he could spit from one platform to the other in the métro (you can just see it, can't you?). He was really of provincial bourgeois extraction, being the heir of a dealer from Rouen. Shortly after he arrived, a rash of subversive songs broke out and there were complaints about the bad food. In other words, G. was a political activist.

S. was a communist too, but less of a fanatic. He was more interested in going for long walks through the town with me than in politics. We started to learn Arabic. G. too made an effort in this direction, anxious as he was to incite the local populace to revolt, but he soon gave up. He found Arabic too medieval and scholastic for his liking. In the evening by candlelight he made up songs about the bean-and-meat rations and the end of military service. After a month or two he disappeared overnight, whisked away by the powers that be. He wrote to us a few weeks later from some godforsaken hole where they were making life difficult for him, because of his little tunes. S. felt no ambition to spread propaganda. We went on learning Arabic. Some areas of the town were so far away that we wondered if we'd ever find our way back.

One day, on the road between Bou Jeloud and Bab Fetouh which skirts the city walls, we met an Arab who was gazing straight ahead, steadfast and motionless. We have come to the end of the prologue. The next I knew I was in Taza. Then in Oudjda. Then in Oran. Then in Marseilles. And then I was in a seedy hotel in Paris. I was working. I was on my own.

It was only several weeks later that I found out that S. was back as well. We arranged to meet in a café in the Place de la

République, the one where the irregular spacing in the urinal caters to customers of varying widths. S. was tickled by this, and fixed the meeting place partly so he could show it to me. He was savoring the picturesque charms of Europe. He had two fat girls in tow, whose only redeeming feature was their semi-sluttishness. Their minds were poorly endowed, and their flesh was not much better, as I found out a few hours later. To start with, S. and I reminisced while the two lumps sat silently. Do you remember, do you remember, Moulay Idris, Moulay Idris?

"You're not going to start talking about A-rabs are you?" said one of those persons.

"I can't stand darkies," said the other. Upon which they rapidly exchanged a few obscene remarks. Then the one sitting opposite me asked:

"Is it true, that story of yours?" We had followed two young girls to one of the furthest town gates. It was getting dark, and an Arab came towards us with a rifle in his hand. S. took us to a small restaurant where he had a slate to chalk up debts. Then there was the story of the young boys who waited for us at night near Bou Jeloud.

"You dirty bastards," said one of the girls.

S. was really having a good time that evening. Maybe he was pleased to see me again and to fix in our minds memories of our army days, memories which will stay with him, unchanged, until he dies. S. wanted the fun to continue, so we went to Luna Park. I realized I was going to have to pay some attention to the broad. We go and have a drink in a café near Porte Maillot. After that S. disappears with the other girl. I start to take the one that's left to her place.

"Sounds great, Africa," says she. No doubt she has in mind certain stories about the sexual prowess of its inhabitants. She moves up closer. I stop the taxi in front of a café-tobacconist's.

"I'm just going to get some cigarettes."

"Get Lucky Strike," says she as though I had asked her opinion.

She was drenched in cheap perfume and it made me feel like throwing up. I got out of the taxi, went into the café, and out through the other door. I got home as fast as I could. I worked until five that morning. At dawn the early buses started going by under my window. At that time I was living near the Stock Exchange in a cheap boardinghouse that got pulled down around about when this story ends. One of S.'s buddies was living there too; it was partly because of him that I was accepted as one of a gang that practiced the art of living without overexerting themselves. Another reason was that, like them, I was not working an eight-hour day; sometimes I worked more than twelve, but they forgave me for that because it didn't bring in any money. I had never felt any desire to mix with down-and-outs, but for over six months they were my only company. These exotic characters held no fascination for me and now I can barely dredge up out of my memory glimpses of a face or echoes of a name. All that was ten years ago. Writing about it is like conjuring up the dead; nothing around me seemed alive and it did not bother me. Indeed, my companions, with their naive uncertainties, were not really living and the only way in which their rejection of convention showed itself was in their use of metaphor and antonomasia. In this field they were uncontested champions, being versed in every figure of speech and verbal device and not hesitating to use them liberally. But the plans they dreamed up were usually just childish; fortunately they didn't often put them into practice, the best plan of all being to do nothing.

The brightest spark among them was a tipster at the races. He combined a certain artful resourcefulness with great gifts of oratory; for the gift of gab, as he said, no one had anything on him. He was one of the first of the gang to treat me like a brother; sometimes I went with him to the races, at Le

Tremblay, at Maisons, all around Paris. Several times I even deigned to act the client who had struck it rich backing a horse at high odds; all I had to do was shake his hand with a knowing look. Then the people standing round in a circle proffered their cash immediately and rushed off to place their bets. We went home by taxi; the day's takings were always good, though the rest of the gang hardly ever won anything. He had no qualms about making a killing while the going was good. After a while I noticed that he had a fat pig of a girlfriend who was . . . guess who. She kept her mouth shut.

Each of these gentlemen had at least one woman. Some of the women lasted only a short time; others, whether out of love or apathy, lasted longer; all either past or future whores. We got together every day in cafés. Our habits were regular, life flowed by sweetly behind the banks of piled-up, empty glasses and slates covered with figures. Mathematical skills were highly appreciated by the gang. When I had finished working—apart from the days when I went to the races with that strange cove Oscar (yes, the tipster was called Oscar and the friend in my boardinghouse was usually known by his surname F., nobody used his first name normally)—then I would go and join them. I only had to cross the square in front of the Stock Exchange, go up the Rue Montmartre, cross the boulevards, then go up the Rue du Faubourg-Montmartre. There they were in the Rue Richer, not far from the Folies-Bergère. I knew how to play cards too. I was no dumber than the next man and more often than not, I won. Some of them cheated so pathetically that it made you wonder how old they were. But what on earth was I doing there? What was I doing there?

Two or three times a month I went to see a relative who had my welfare at heart. I used to call him "uncle," though maybe I should have called him "auntie." He turned one or two of my childhood friends into real pansies. His house was full of cheap ornaments from his time in the colonies. He classified countries according to their longitude; for him the Orient was to the east, and Morocco was the same as Brittany. As far as I was concerned, I was sure I'd been in the Orient; this gave us something to talk about. Every month he gave me some money, a small allowance, just enough to look after my basic needs; they were very modest. Thus relieved of material worries, I was able to devote all my time to unpaid work. As I was leaving this gentleman's house one day in September, I met the tipster's girlfriend with another woman I must have seen somewhere, because she looked as if she recognized me. I didn't inquire what they were doing in the neighborhood. The conversation went more or less as follows:

"Where you going?"

"Oh, just going for a walk," I said.

"You going to see Oscar?"

"Not specially," I said, or, "Not specifically."

"You don't seem to like telling people where you're going."

"Um . . ." I said, my voice tailing off at the end into dots . . .

"That's the bastard that ditched me with 17 francs 50 on the taximeter."

"Oscar won't do that to you," I said.

"What a thing to do. It was 17 francs 50, damn it."

"Come off it," I said, "you don't imagine that I'm going to pay you back for the damn taxi, do you?"

I was learning how to treat women.

"What a jerk."

She was getting on her high horse. Her friend said, "Here you are." They stopped. I went as far as the sidewalk. They said good-bye to each other.

"I'm going to wait across the street," said the woman that I thought I'd seen before. On the other side of the road was a small café.

"Ah," I said.

"You going to Marcel's afterwards?"

Marcel's was another small café, where Oscar, my co-boarder, S. and two or three other rogues and their women all got together.

"Not particularly."

"Why don't you stay and keep me company?"

"All right."

In the half-light of the café loomed the inert shapes of some tables and chairs, a billiard table, a pay phone and the waiter who came to take our orders.

"She goes a couple of times a week," she told me, "he's an old banker: she thinks he'll leave her something, he's about seventy."

"Some people aren't choosy," I said.

"Perhaps you'd rather she worked in a factory eight hours a day? That doesn't stop you from having to go on the streets."

"No, I know," I said.

"What about you, do you work?"

"At least I don't live off prostitution."

"But do you work?"

"Yes, of course I do."

"Eight hours a day?"

"Ten, twelve, sometimes more."

"Tell me another."

"It's the truth: I do at least ten hours sometimes."

"Where?"

"At home."

"Does it bring in a lot?"

"Nothing at all."

She stared at me.

"Just as I suspected," she said.

"What did you suspect?"

"You must be a writer."

No, I wasn't a writer; I explained to her what I did. She

listened to me carefully; she seemed to understand. I got carried away with my subject: myself; I stopped abruptly. What sense could she possibly make of what I was telling her? I can't remember what we talked about after that. Her friend came back; they went off alone to Marcel's: of course, that's right, that's what it was called, I thought I'd forgotten. I went off in a different direction, walking the streets of the city and going nowhere special.

From one street corner to the next, I ended up at home with a sandwich in my pocket and a bottle of wine under my arm. While I ate and drank, I got down to work, and that evening, I remember very well, I couldn't get anything done. The mistakes lined up in rows several deep, and I got discouraged. I emptied the bottle, then another that I had at home, got bombed out of my mind, then went to sleep. Everything suddenly seemed to have been blotted out. But the next morning, at the crack of dawn, I was back behind the plough, tilling my barren land, as stubbornly as an ox or a mule. A few days later I was being interrogated by somebody else.

He was with G. I met them late one October afternoon, in the Rue Vivienne, I think it was. They were out for a stroll. I hadn't seen G. since he got sent away in the Rif; we had tried to see each other since he'd been back in Paris, but he was so involved with politics that he never seemed able to fix a definite meeting. He wrote and told me that "his time was completely taken up." He had ended up being something quite important in the Party. The only newspapers I read were folded in eight and pinned to a wall, so I found that out by accident. Well, I bumped into him by chance. He said how pleased he was to see me, and slapped me on the back. His companion didn't want to know me at first. We talked about the army, the colonies, politics. G.'s specialty now was anti-military action; he was under the threat of several months in jail.

The other guy suddenly said, "But when you were over there, you could have been forced to shoot at Moroccans."

"That's right," I said.

"And what would you have done?"

"That's a tricky question," I said.

G. changed the subject: "Don't you want to come to the meeting at the Vel d'hiv this evening?"

"Doriot will be speaking," the comrade said.

Doriot did indeed speak. It was fantastic, no doubt about it. The comrade sang lustily; I didn't know the words. I just listened and looked. G. had left us to do whatever it was he had to do. Suddenly, when it was all over, we found ourselves side by side, the comrade and I, over near Grenelle, on the Left Bank, in the dark. We chatted.

"Do you belong to the Party?"

"No, do you?"

"No, I'm a supporter."

"Yeah, I'm a supporter too."

"But you don't belong."

"No, politics is not my game."

"Politics don't come into it. What matters is the Revolution."

"Ah yes, of course that's right, the Revolution."

"So, why don't you join?"

"It's not as simple as that."

"I see."

"No, it's not as simple as you might think, especially for a poet."

"You're a poet?"

"Yes, I'm Saxel."

"Excuse me?"

"I said: I'm Saxel."

"Oh! Saxel." He looked at me.

"Do *you* write?"

"No. At least it depends what you mean by that."

"Well, you're not a writer—a poet, a playwright, a novelist, a journalist, an art critic?"

"I'm none of those."

"But you're an intellectual."

"I'd be satisfied with just being intelligent."

"You admire intelligence a lot?"

"That's an understatement."

We went on discussing. He scorned intelligence, or so he claimed. I went his way, we reached Montparnasse and he suggested a drink; he was outraged by what he called my "intellectualism" but he still wanted to go on talking. We sat down among a huge crowd of people, my second for the evening.

"There are some weird types here," I said.

"Is it the first time you've been here?"

"Yes, it is."

He barely managed to hide his disappointment: what kind of little social democrat twerp had he picked up? I didn't know what to say. Someone stopped at our table and exchanged a few words with Saxel. A few banalities were uttered. The man went off; he was dressed in velvet.

"That's Vladislav, the painter," Saxel said to me.

"Ah, ah," I said.

"Have you heard of him?"

"I think so," I said. Saxel looked at me. Where on earth had I been all my life? We downed several beers.

"There's more than one world, you know," I said to him, "there isn't only the world that you see or that you think you see, or that you imagine you see, the world that the blind feel, that the armless hear and the deaf smell, this world of objects and forces, of things solid or illusory, this world of life and death, of birth and destruction, this world where we drink and in which we go to sleep. There's at least one more than I know of: the world of numbers and figures, of identities and functions, of operations and groups, of sets and spaces. There are people, as you know, who hold that these are only abstractions, combinations and constructs of the mind. They would have us believe in a sort of architecture; elements are taken from nature, refined, polished, dried out, and then used as bricks by the human mind to build a magnificent mansion, as an eloquent testimony to the power of reason. You must be familiar with this idea, it's a popular theory that your own philosophy teacher must have had. A building, they see mathematics as a building! You make sure the foundations are solid before you build the first floor, and when you've built the first floor, you move on to the second floor, and then the third, and so on, and it just goes on and on. But things aren't actually like that; you shouldn't compare geometry and calculus to building houses or walls, but to botany, to geography or even to the physical sciences. It's about describing a world, discovering it, not about constructing or inventing it, because it exists outside the human mind and independently of it. What you have to do is explore this universe and then report to mankind on what you've seen there—I said 'seen' on purpose. But to report on it, you need a language: the language of signs and formulas, which is usually taken for the very essence of science but is in fact only its means of expression. This language is even more powerless to describe the riches of the mathematical world than French is to articulate the multiplicity of things about us, because they are not of the same order of being. I mean there's a sort of mathematical philology, that is called logic. But maybe I'm boring you?"

"It's just that I don't altogether follow you," replied Saxel.

"I'd have to give you some examples."

"It might be too complicated."

"No, not at all. There's one that always comes up, the one about the algebraic equations with one unknown."

"Pooh, equations," said Saxel.

"Ah," I retorted, "I bet you're one of those people, waiter

another beer, who boast about not understanding mathematics, who pride themselves on getting stuck on the square of the hypotenuse."

"That's me," said Saxel.

"Doesn't it bother you?"

"Should it?"

"Of course. What satisfaction can you get from not understanding something?"

"OK, let's go back to your equations."

"You're not sick of the whole thing?"

"I'll try not to puke."

"Do you know what it means to solve an equation?"

"I think so."

"Tell me then."

"Uh. It means finding the value of the unknown."

"How?"

"By making calculations."

"Yes, but which?"

"Well, addition, subtraction, multiplication and division."

"And. . . ?"

"There are more than four?"

"I believe so."

"Oh yeah, that's right, you can find the square root of a number, like Cosinus did."

"Which is the opposite of raising a number to the power of whatever."

"You could make great puns out of all these expressions."

"You make puns?"

"Natch, you gotta keep up with the times. Let's get back to your fucking equations, waiter, another beer."

"How many steps will it take you to calculate your unknown quantity?"

"What do you mean, how many?"

"Well, how many?"

17

"How should I know?"

"A finite number or an infinite number?"

"An infinite number: that's a good one, would you ever have time?"

"That's down-to-earth, common-sense speaking. But I might tell you that in calculus, for example, you're dealing all the time with expressions that imply an infinite number of operations."

"I stand corrected."

"But since we're talking about algebraic operations, we'll stick to the realm of algebra and we'll only think of a solution using a finite number of algebraic operations and more specifically radicals."

"Bunch of crooks, these radicals."

"What?"

"Nothing, nothing. I'm getting damned interested. Damned interested. Let's go on?"

"Let's go on. So, where do you start from?"

"Easy! From what you know."

"From known quantities."

"That's what I said."

"Right. Now that we've got a clear idea of what solving an equation means, let's try and solve a first-degree equation."

"That's child's play," exclaimed Saxel, "you only have to divide. I know all about that, I learned it from a drunk teacher whose beard smelled of snuff, pooh! it was disgusting. I was always first in math at school you know."

"Did you go as far as a second-degree equation, then?"

"Of course I did! Minus bee plus or minus the square root of bee two minus four aycee over two, there, that's it! Slurp, slurp, slurp, slurp, this beer's good."

"And what do you notice about that formula?"

"I'm really getting clever: the square root. The square root, that's what I notice. And now I see what you're getting at: it's clear as crystal, it's simple, it's beautiful. For the third degree you have to take the cube root, for the fourth degree the fourth root, for the fifth degree the fifth root, and so on. It's logical, isn't it. Logically simple."

"No, after the fifth degree, it doesn't work."

"Why ever not?"

"There's no way of solving equations above the fifth degree by using algebra, except in very special cases. It doesn't work for most equations."

"Perhaps no one knows how to go about it."

"It's been proved."

"But that's preposterous!"

"You're right. It's preposterous because there's a reality which is not amenable to algebraic logic, because there's a reality which is beyond us and which we can't explain using language invented by the rational mind, because the rational mechanism for reconstructing that world fails. Just as the mechanism for a rational reconstruction of this world fails too, I suppose. But don't think that it all stops there and that the intelligence of man has given up trying to explore it. It comes up against an obstacle, it tries to get over it, and gets around it with a new theory, group theory, which reveals new wonders. I'm sure a powerful mind could conceive of this reality in a flash; our own inadequacy forces us to rely on trick solutions."

"It's damned idealist, all this, you know."

"Realist you mean! Numbers are real. Numbers exist! They're as real as this talk, more real than the philosophers' everlasting table, infinitely more real than this table wham!"

"Could you make less noise please," said the waiter.

"No one asked you anything," said Saxel.

"We can't hear anything but you two talking," said the waiter.

"You could be a bit more polite," said Saxel.

"We're asking you to make less noise," said the waiter.

19

"I shall make as much noise as I like," said Saxel.

Another waiter came over, then another, then the manager, then another waiter as well. Once we were outside, we started to walk off into the night.

"What a lousy joint," said Saxel, "what a dump."

He was wiping his hat with his jacket sleeve. My mind was sparking. We walked down Boulevard Raspail. "Real," I said, "they're real," then Rue du Bac as far as the Seine. The moon was floating on the water. Before me there was an Arab, motionless. I am on the road between Bou Jeloud and Bab Fetouh, there's an escutcheon shaped in the mud, a passing cloud on blue.

It rained a lot that winter; from November to February the weather was mild and wet, nice weather for fish, and in the rain I often went for walks, sometimes alone, sometimes with Saxel, sometimes with the woman that I had met one day with Oscar's blonde friend. Do you remember, the drops of water made her black raincoat shiny and we ended up taking refuge in some outlying bistro and coming back on the trolley, slow and noisy. From the very first day we went out together, I got over my surprise that I could talk about myself and even more that I could listen to what someone else had to say. My eyes still blinked when I looked at the world, but at least I looked. My ears buzzed, my hands trembled, I was emerging from the water meted out by the sky, from the earth with its smouldering fire as I watched and listened to the Seine flow under the bridges. The first time, we went along the embankments as far as the Place Valhubert and, from there, we went into the twelfth arrondissement.

"Look, this is where I became a soldier," I said in front of the barracks at Reuilly, and I recounted my memories of military service, which I won't do here a second time, have no fear. Another time, I showed her the house where I was born: through the streets of Paris, I was reclaiming my memory. I was forced to recognize what I wanted to forget: so one day she commented:

"Don't you have any family?"

I don't know how it came up. I replied:

"I have an uncle who gives me a small allowance. I was leaving his house that time when we first met."

My reply did not satisfy her. A bit later, I said to her:

"It's a sad story, I was abandoned." Did I look as if I was joking?

"Yes, my parents abandoned me, left me on the street, dumped me on a doorstep, with nowhere to go: I was eighteen at the time."

As I remember, we were just going along the Quai de Valmy. We stopped to look at the canal, at least I think it was that time.

"You may think it sounds like a stupid story, well, my parents threw me out because I failed an exam. You won't believe it, because I didn't get into Polytechnique. My father's lifelong ambition was for me to get into Polytechnique, it's ridiculous isn't it? Well you see, I didn't get in. And so I found myself out in the street, literally in the street.

"The only thing is," I added, "that I'm not telling the truth. It's bad to lie, isn't it? The whole thing is even more ridiculous than you think: because I didn't exactly fail the exam. Shall we go to the Buttes-Chaumont? I cheated actually. It was a huge scandal. My father is a very respectable gentleman: he thought his honor was at stake. They shut the gates of learning in my face. A silly story, don't you think?"

"But whatever made you. . . ?"

"How do I know? Something came over me, I suddenly got the idea. What can I do about it now, no one will ever be interested in what I do, I'm an outcast, you see, to people who've never made any stupid mistakes; that's how it should be, don't you think? Anyway I don't think about it anymore, it's not worth it. My silly behavior will stay with me all my life.

These things belong to childhood, but the consequences stay with you. Nothing is forgotten and no one forgives: that's the rule. Only, only, what on earth shall I do with my life? Tell me."

Of course I did not talk about that sort of thing with Saxel, it stuck in my throat, so I preferred to inculcate in him some notions of differential and integral calculus. He got me reading poetry, his own, as well as little booklets produced by his friends that I first of all took for theosophical publications. But I soon realized that they were looking forward more to the arrival of the Antichrist than to that of the white horse. And in order to bring about the liberation of the Mind and of the proletariat, they preached an "infrapsychically and subconsciously based" mixture of metapsychism, of dialectical materialism, and of "primitive mentality." All of which surprised me less, however, than the resounding praises being sung of one Anglarès, the leader of this group, who, it was hinted, was entrusted with a prodigious and historic mission, and who Saxel informed me was a medical doctor by profession. Since it was the first time I had had anything to do with some of the many disciplines across which his friends ranged, from chiromancy to Stalinism, via Papusism and criminology, I had to ask Saxel for some explanations. But rather than enlightening me at the doctrinal level, he chose to tell me about Anglarès's life, which was full of mysteries and strange incidents, and about Anglarès's friends, whose lives were just as amazing, or else he would describe the lives of their enemies and opponents, which were indescribably awful. Anglarès did indeed have working against him a certain number of rival groupings, made up, or so he said —and Saxel repeated it—of cops and queers. This was how Saxel got me ready to "make contact," as he put it.

Most of the winter went by before Saxel thought me ready. He spoke of it once in a while, every so often, then quite frequently. One day he made up his mind:

"Would you like to come to the Place de la République with

me at noon?"

The pavement café in the Place de la République was the meeting place for Anglarès and some of the more noteworthy of his noteworthy friends: in fact, they all thought themselves noteworthy, as I was to find out later. Among the people scattered around the tables I immediately identified the person that everyone had come for: you could spot Anglarès a mile off. He had very long hair; he was wearing a huge black felt hat and a pince-nez tied to his left ear by a wide ribbon. He would have looked like an old-fashioned photographer except for the red tie which indicated that he was up with the times. The young people around him, on the other hand, seemed perfectly normal: they were all about my age, whereas Anglarès looked noticeably older.

When we arrived, everyone was already deep in conversation over drinks. Saxel introduced me. Anglarès took off his pince-nez to greet me: he uttered a few kind words. The others looked at me: some indifferently, others with obvious suspicion. We sat down. The waiter hurried over to ask what we wanted. Anglarès was good enough to tell me what they had been talking about before. Near the soda fountain I saw a strange-looking stone. They had been talking about that. Anglarès had just acquired it from a secondhand shop in Belleville, both because of its interesting shape and also because of certain unusual circumstances surrounding its discovery—and what amazing circumstances they were. The stone bore quite a strong resemblance to a crocodile. Now, the day before, Anglarès, on the advice of the woman with whom he "was smitten" (as he told me later), had consulted a clairvoyant. In her crystal ball, this clairvoyant, he said, had seen a "crocodile going downstairs."

"I thought that she was referring to that creep Salton."

Anglarès attributed anything bad that happened to him to the evil influence of this person, the leader of a rival group.

"But, as you can see, this is what she was referring to."

The disciples looked at the stone in silence.

"And then, yesterday evening, the crocodile appeared to me again. Looking up a quotation in the poems of Théoclaste d'Avidya, I came across the two lines that all of you must know: 'The flaccid crocodile with coral teeth / Teeters unhurried down Montmirail Street.' I had never analyzed those lines in any detail. Yesterday, I don't know why, I was really struck by them. I felt them reverberate through my unconscious: you understand what I mean. And this morning as I was walking down the Rue de Montmirail, I saw this crocodile in a second-hand shop window, which turned these premonitions into a concrete reality. You'll have noticed that, according to Théoclaste d'Avidya, and according to the clairvoyant, I was the one going slowly down the Rue de Montmirail, so I'm the crocodile."

Someone (the one called Vachol) said:

"Your unconscious has revealed your totem to you . . ."

He tailed off into silence. Anglarès smiled at his well-meaning disciple. This approving look gave rise to excited comments from the other spectators. Some said that the crocodile was such a noble creature that anyone who had given any thought to the matter would have realized that you couldn't possibly associate that creep Edouard Salton with such a magnificent beast. Others were holding forth on the nature of chance, on reptilians, on the Rue de Montmirail, on the repetition of "teeth teeters," on the use of imperfect rhyme *(loc. cit.)*, on the divinatory practices of Théoclaste d'Avidya and various other details which bore more or less relevance to the topic under discussion. Anglarès listened without saying a word and sipped his aperitif. Saxel kept quiet: he looked about the same age as Anglarès.

At one o'clock sharp, Anglarès put the venerable stone crocodile in his pocket, paid for his drink and got up, followed by Vachol. He was going to have lunch; Vachol was going to join him. The others went their own ways. Saxel left with a young man with a high forehead. I was left alone with two bills that someone absentmindedly forgot to pay. Saxel must have been laboring under a delusion if he thought that these gentlemen would be interested in me. Or perhaps that is a new boy's introduction: you have to pay for the drinks. I wasn't very impressed with the careless way they left their bills lying around. But it was obvious that becoming a member of the group was not plain sailing. The question of the bill was just a defense mechanism. Small groups close in on themselves like clams squirted with lemon juice.

At least such were my thoughts as I went to Marcel's. The gang was just finishing lunch. They were going off together to the Vincennes races along with someone that I didn't know. I let them get on with their business and sat down. I was left with the women. They were chattering away, but I didn't hear them. I stared at the mustard pot, I experienced its volume in space, I projected it onto the tablecloth and onto the old-fashioned cylinder of a bottle of red wine. One of the women, called Manon (it's true, really it is), opened her bag, powdered her nose and without looking round asked me:

"Have you seen Odile today?"

"No, I haven't seen her."

"No one's seen her for the last couple of days."

That made me smile because I thought of the pun "the cracodile cracks Odile" and the stone.

"Do you know something we don't?"

Trust women to get ideas straight away.

"Me? Of course not."

But I couldn't help chuckling at the pun.

"Are you a little sweet on her?" asked Oscar's woman.

"Wadjamean: sweet?" I asked.

"Oh, come on, don't play dumb."

I finished my Camembert without deigning to reply. Two of

the women got up; they had work to do in the neighborhood. The third stayed; it wasn't Manon (I can't help it, that really was her name), nor Oscar's woman. It was Adèle. Oscar's woman was called Alice. Adèle said to me:

"Mind if I have a coffee with you?"

Two coffees were brought. Marcel, the owner, idly watched the passersby. The waiter went and sat down at the end of the bench and started writing a letter; he had a wife and three kids with his mother in the country, as he had told me more than once.

"You're in love with that chick, aren't you?" Adèle asked.

"That what?"

"You know. I'm talking about Odile."

"Crac-crac-Odile," I replied.

"If you were interested . . ." she began.

"I get your meaning," I said, interrupting her and calling the waiter.

"Look," she said insistently, "don't you ever . . ."

"I'm not interested in love."

She shrugged her shoulders.

"People say that."

It was around three. I went home to my mathematical calculations. Around five I got a message. Anglarès was inviting me to dinner. Right then I felt more like seeing Odile. The numbers whizzed across the page. When I heard the evening papers being sold, I sprinkled some water on my hair, gave my nails a quick cleaning and went out. Feeling a bit wobbly and unsure of the way, I set off. I went the long way round to call at Marcel's. Two of the gang were playing cards. They were claiming that "the others had made a killing and had gone on a binge." I hesitated about Anglarès's invitation: no doubt it would have been more fun to spend the evening with Oscar. But I went on my way and, around seven o'clock, got to the Place de la République. It struck me that this was where I'd met S. after we got back from Morocco.

There were at least half a dozen more people having a drink that evening than there had been at lunchtime. New introductions were made. Saxel was a bit drunk. He didn't seem to recognize me anymore. Anglarès addressed a few gracious words in my direction again. They were all talking about that famous crocodile, and those who hadn't had a chance to admire it that morning were lamenting the fact. About eight o'clock, Anglarès said to me:

"I'd be pleased if you could join us for dinner tonight."

It was going to be a big party, judging by the number of people who piled into the taxi to go up to the Buttes-Chaumont. Apart from Saxel and the ever-faithful Vachol, the young man with the high forehead got in as well, and so did a sixth character who had nothing special to recommend him that I could see then. Everyone apart from me was in good spirits, declaring themselves to be strongly against teetotalitarianism (just as they were against vegetarianism and chastity), all of which seemed to set them apart from members of the other sects that I had come across.

Anglarès lived in a harmless-looking suburban house, the sort of residence you would expect of a doctor on the outskirts of town. If the outside was unremarkable, it was obvious as soon as you stepped inside that its inhabitant was someone out of the ordinary. It immediately made you think of the hideout of a fortune-teller or an Oriental seer. We went into a large room which was used as a dining room, reception room and work room, insofar as any work was done there at all. There were impressive pictures hanging on the walls. A whole lot of equipment which I couldn't figure out was carefully laid out on shelves made of some exotic wood or other. There was also, of course, a sizeable collection of books. I glanced at them but the names meant nothing to me. Anglarès offered us another drink, which prompted the entry of two ladies, one his wife, the other the mistress of one of the guests: I couldn't figure out which at first and it didn't really matter. Eight of us sat down at the dining-room table; Anglarès rang a small silver bell with a church-like sound and the first course arrived amidst witty and profound remarks, everyone at the table trying to produce a gem to outshine their neighbor.

After dinner, people lit up, and everyone's attention turned to me. I understood that this party had somehow been thrown in my honor, or my dishonor, depending on whether or not I got caught in the web of questions that these people were spinning.

"I have always had a poor opinion of mathematics," said Anglarès, "but I have to admit that it has its uses, such as calculating probabilities, insofar as this provides a scientific basis for astrology."

"I've never been into that," I said, "I've never been interested in applied mathematics."

"Mathematics is so cold and dehumanized," said Madame Anglarès.

"It is my life," I replied.

"Don't you worry about becoming dehumanized?"

"No, I'm not too worried about that."

The two ladies shrugged their shoulders with extreme disdain and began to chitchatter between themselves.

"He's very human because he's a poet, and he's a poet because he's a mathematician," said Saxel benignly.

"A poet is he," exclaimed Anglarès, "you're rather jumping to conclusions," and then he said in an agreeable tone: "We should like to know more."

It was an invitation to hold forth.

"It's not easy," I said, "I don't know how to go about explaining to you the beauty of automorphous functions or even the less complicated conic sections. You have to go into it in depth, otherwise it's just so many words."

There was a silence. I suppose I must have started to sound pretentious, but I already had a reputation to uphold. I went on:

"A kind of . . ."

I hesitated:

". . . harmonious architecture."

"What we're interested in," said Saxel, "is not that, but what you've sometimes told me about the failure of rational constructs."

"Which cannot get to the bottom of a different reality."

"That's right."

"The rational logical symbolism that we use cannot account for all the complexity of mathematics, nor can it express it. I could quote you a lot of examples."

"Are you claiming that mathematics is a construct of the human mind?" someone asked.

"More precisely, I'm saying that the object of mathematics is not a construct of the human mind. It's more like botany or ethnography. You explore it, you don't construct it."

"All this is really very interesting," said Anglarès, giving his pince-nez a wipe.

I wondered how much he was understanding. He tried to get things straight.

"But basically what are you exploring?"

"The world of mathematical reality."

"And how do you explore it?"

"In every possible way."

"And you say that this world is beyond the grasp of reason?"

"I think it is."

"So there must be a sort of mathematical unconscious," said my interlocutor with great satisfaction, and straight away addressing himself to the others, he announced, "This is yet another triumph over reason; the unconscious will win on every front."

This news aroused general enthusiasm; even the two ladies took part in it. Their approval was like getting a good grade; I did not bother to correct the misrepresentations of my ideas, or rather the ideas that I was clumsily trying to express. Vachol gave a friendly, almost tender look in my direction.

"It's a sign," he was saying. "There's a Revolution of the Mind taking place in every discipline."

Saxel was proud of me. I had a feeling that the others were sulking, at least the young man with the high forehead was (his name was Louis Chènevis, as I found out later that same evening), and, as for the sixth passenger whose name was Vincent N., he was showing a distinct lack of enthusiasm for this new voyage of discovery. And so Chènevis and N. were sulking, and Saxel was proud of me and that yes-man Vachol was nodding his approval. They seemed to be going to extremes. Anglarès was intent on annexing territory for the greater glory of his name. Pursuing the line of least resistance, he asked me:

"And chance? Isn't there an element of chance in mathematics?"

I tried to think of an appropriate answer: "Every number is the sum of at most nine cubes."

My audience did not bat an eyelash on hearing this statement. Anglarès listened attentively and Saxel smiled like a man already in the know.

"It's a theorem," I added. "It can be proved, but what is not proved is that there are only two numbers that need exactly nine cubes. Those are 23 and 239. We don't know if there are others. But you can prove that there is a finite number of them."

"I can't see an element of chance in that," said Anglarès.

"No. But there's no obvious reason why it should be like that."

"No reason? Which proves there's something like a mathematical unconscious."

30

I didn't answer. Anglarès was satisfied. So was I. We talked about other things.

At midnight there was some movement which made me think that it must be time to go home; but I was wrong, for the evening was moving towards its climax.

"Alice, please bring me today's envelope," Anglarès said, sitting at his desk.

Everyone gathered round him. After a few minutes Madame Anglarès came back into the room with an envelope sealed with five silvery wax seals. Anglarès grabbed it and held it out.

"Who wants to open it?"

The date, now yesterday's, was written on the envelope in a small, tidy hand. Saxel took the message and amid complete silence he broke the seals, unfolded a sheet of paper and read out something along the following lines:

Predictions for the 18/7/x—. The grass has died in the field of steel where the cucumbers drink. Have you seen the cloud of sunshades exhaled by the infinite air of the summits? Come and swim in the oceans tamed by many zephyrs and slowly crossed by officers whose teeth are green with seaweed. I can see the sabers growing on the nine dice that the divine multiples offer to astrologers. Back on these shores where our forefathers died a man was advancing armed with slow horses.

"It's a beautiful poem," said Saxel breaking the silence.

"Will you never stop seeing everything from a literary point of view?" retorted Chènevis in an irritated voice.

Anglarès took the paper back and read it carefully; Vachol leaned over his shoulder. Without a doubt he believed that he was putting himself in touch with occult powers.

"It's phenomenal," he muttered after a while.

Everyone looked at him.

"Have you got an interpretation for it?"

"It's child's play," he replied with a smile.

He gave the prognosticator a knowing look:

"You explain it to them," said Anglarès, who looked to me as if he understood it less than Vachol.

"It's child's play but at the same time it's phenomenal! The two sabers are the two numbers that our friend spoke of earlier. The nine dice are obviously the nine cubes of which they are the sum. The astrologers are the mathematicians and the divine multiples are all the numbers. The shores where our forefathers died, that's mathematics because we did not know up until now what an important part the unconscious plays in it. The man advancing is our friend once more and the slow horses with which he is armed are rational proofs. There you are."

"Very impressive," said Anglarès.

"So when did you make up this message?" asked Saxel.

"Fifteen days ago," replied Anglarès. "At that time I wasn't thinking about mathematics at all."

"It's one of your best predictions," said Chènevis.

"Vachol is certainly the best psychic analyst among us," said Anglarès.

"It was self-evident," said Vachol.

I was a bit taken aback, because I couldn't work out where the catch was.

"But how do you interpret the beginning?" asked Vincent N.

"It's redundant text," replied Anglarès.

"Naturally," said his buddy, "isn't the rest enough for you?"

I basked in a bit of reflected glory. Then we took our leave. Chènevis and his lady went off towards Montmartre. The others, including myself, walked down towards the Place de la République with the intention of having a beer before going our separate ways.

I am still sometimes sitting down with them as I see these images, but they are scenes that grow dimmer all the time because of the layers of indifference under which they lie buried. And I certainly no longer remember what was said that night, even though the memory of that first evening at Anglarès's house has stayed with me quite vividly, for me to be able to harness it in a coherent narration and dialogue. After that first meeting comes a period of obscurity where I can no longer place details in a chronological order but where characters come to me all at once or I remember the rather more unusual events without being able to recall how they came about or developed. How can I speak about the way my relationship with one or another person began and evolved, when they are no more to me now than slightly shifting statues that stir slightly, no more than minimally mobile robots that move a fraction, like puppets whose rib cages can fill out to give the impression of human breath? I'm not using the words *robot* and *puppet* to denigrate these people who have been erased from my life. Of myself as I was then, I have retained only the image of a fairground toy, the mediocre slow-motion demonstration of a reality that escaped me then. At the same time, I would not try to deny that these people were living then, as I was. Looking back I do not think badly of them for the parts they played.

I seem to remember that, in the beginning, Saxel had to press me before I would go back either to the café in the Place de la République or to Anglarès's house, where everyone met two or three evenings a week around midnight. I wasn't used to their ways yet, slightly put off by them, and anyway I was still frequenting my friends in the Rue de Montmartre, partly out of natural inertia and no doubt also partly out of a liking for Odile. I've put inertia before liking because I could have seen Odile without playing cards with those characters, without going to the races with Oscar, and without listening for hours and hours to S.'s stories about his illicit dealings, all of which were not really to my taste, but which were part of my life, lost cause that it was. That spring, because spring it was, I kept working as well, getting lost in never-ending research. I could not see the end of it and, even if I had found a solution, how would I have let the world of learning know? In this respect I lived in total isolation, and any publication arising out of my research was destined to oblivion, as eminently forgettable as winning at billiards or cup-and-ball. But I was not worried by any of the consequences of what I was doing, for I lived without thinking, having given up all hope of happier days. However, that spring, for there was a spring that year like every year, I began to feel less confident about the hopelessness of my own life and less certain about my own unhappy fate. The feeling that someone might one day listen to me was more important than the feeling that I was someone, or nearly someone, in the eyes of other people, like Saxel. When I tried to articulate my thoughts, it was a travesty that came back to me, nothing but a distorted reflection, but at least it was something different, whether better or worse, than living in a total lack of communication. I had something to hope for now, albeit something very minor; to get a distorted reflection was better than nothing at all. I was forced out of the quietude into which despair had led me, out of my passive state, out of my "happiness."

In times that followed, I sometimes found myself suddenly looking back and lamenting the loss of those tranquil days when I used to bury myself in everlasting mathematical calculations, living near the poverty line, with childish, gullible down-and-outs as my only occasional company. The boundaries of their world were so narrow that even the next neighborhood was foreign territory to them. They bolstered their happiness with numbers of *La Veine,* betting and broads, befogged by cheap tobacco smoke as they puffed inanely on interminable cigarette butts. Assuming that I had no future, I had built my void upon their nothingness. Later, when I became something, or almost, I recalled some very mellow moments, leaving my lodgings at nightfall, and crossing the Faubourg-Montmartre to meet my buddies in a back room of the café in the Rue Richer where we had so many good games of cards, mellow moments cocooned in decay and muffled by neglect. But over and above all that, there was my friendship with Odile, which was making me more and more uncertain of my own unhappy fate. I no longer forged blindly ahead like a projectile. Little by little I was emerging from the darkness into which I had stumbled with my eyes closed.

The women who frequented Marcel's were all prostitutes. Until then I had never asked myself what Odile was doing with them. It took a while before I noticed that she was the girl-friend of Oscar's brother, a wayward character called Shard, like a broken bottle. Louis Shard only came to Paris every so often, and his visits were always a big event. He was a very important person. He was spoken of in tones of hushed admiration, even fear, and no one ever gossiped at his expense. This made Odile independent and respected, but she stayed in with this set for the same reason as I did: neither of us had budged an inch from the spot where we had been struck down. Where the storm had lain us down, there we remained, quite different from the leaves that are blown about by the winds.

"I don't look around me anymore," she used to say, "not up or down. Nowhere. I just go where I'm going: nowhere. Like you."

"Like me, yes. Like me, you're right."

"We're good friends then, are we?"

"Yes, we're good friends," I said. And then: "Well, that's something." And then again: "Are you in love with that guy?"

"There was a time when I hated him."

That too was something; further on we sat down outside a large café, in the sun.

"Isn't Shard jealous?"

"Why should he be, since we're just good friends?"

35

"He might not understand."

"He's not as bad as all that."

"Isn't he? The others say he is."

"Perhaps he is with them."

"But not with you?"

"He's changed a lot, poor kid."

I can see his head leaning towards hers: full of tender thoughts, the big skinny crook. His hands are like boxers', wooden hands with fingers that crack, and thick hair right down his arms to his knuckles. He prides himself on never carrying a weapon; there is something moving about his toughness; his face fades. Odile is silent, her mind on something else. A little later we met Saxel. "We" included Adèle and Oscar; Oscar was rolling in it, as the saying went that year, and had invited us to a film and a beer afterwards. Saxel went past and saw me. I waved to him.

"Who's that?" asked Oscar.

"A friend of mine."

"Call him over. He can have a drink with us," said Oscar.

"He looks rather snazzy," said Shard, meaning he's well-dressed.

I got up and ran after Saxel.

"Do you want to come and join us?"

"That would be nice, I was out for a walk. Who are you with?"

"Friends of mine. The one on the right's a tipster and the one on the left's his brother, I don't know exactly what he does. Anyway, better not ask. Coming?"

Saxel followed me, intrigued.

"A friend of mine," I said to the others.

He shook hands and sat down.

"Nice evening," said Oscar, and a few moments went by when no one said anything else, and actually it *was* a nice evening: the buds were budding under the electric lights.

36

Saxel, posing as a contributor to *La Veine,* was delighted to make the acquaintance of dropouts and pimps; he was so delighted that he started going to the races with Oscar as well as playing cards seriously. He got quite carried away by his enthusiasm, while I tripled in prestige in his eyes, both because I kept such strange company and because I had kept quiet about it. Word got around the Place de la République and the Buttes-Chaumont as well. Anglarès uttered a few well-disposed words about the lumpenproletariat and Vachol started secretly learning how to play cards. So falling flat on my face was helping me to find my feet. When I rubbed my nose in the dirt, everyone cheered: they thought it was my way of baring my teeth.

By popular demand, I wrote a short article for the *Review of Infrapsychic Research* on the intrinsically objective nature of mathematics, an article, moreover, in which I allowed myself to modify my ideas a little to please the leader of the sect, who published this lavish review thanks to the subsidy given by a woman of nobility, as if the last function of the last woman of the last nobility was to provide the last subsidies for the last reviews. As a result of this article, which was extremely well received, everyone wanted to get to know me. So I was invited to dinner with the Countess de ——, who had acquired her *de* relatively recently. Reluctant to arrive on my own, I arranged to go with Saxel, who was also invited. He came for me in a taxi and we stopped on the way for a fortifier.

"I don't really feel like going," I said.

"You're nervous?"

"No, of course not. I find it a drag."

"You wait, she's a charming lady. Anglarès is in love with her: she knows every medium in Paris. I don't think she's in love with him. In fact, she's leading him on, the bitch. She went and looked him up one day because an article of his had something to do with her, or so she said. That really impressed him. He's been running after her ever since. And she's flattered, naturally."

"I don't really feel like it."

"Oh, come on. You'll see, the food's disgusting. No one has discovered if that's because of avarice or asceticism." I was disgusted with Saxel for gossiping and felt very miserable as I went into this lady's lovely house a few kilometers outside Paris. I let Saxel pay for the taxi.

I saw Anglarès straight away, standing under the lights, and not far away were five or six characters whose names I did not catch even when they were introduced; then at last, the countess. She was quite a pretty woman, eccentrically dressed, at least I thought so; and even those who were more used to it than I must have thought so too. She pronounced a few words that were so to the point that it made me believe that she was well-versed in math, and I was dumbfounded; from behind me, Saxel paid her a compliment. Then I drank cocktails out of small glasses. We left her house very late and I could not help being surprised by what I had seen and heard. As I had begun to get interested in the world, I mean "the external world," I couldn't wait to ask Saxel certain things. One of the guests, one of those whose names I didn't catch, dropped us off at the Place de l'Opéra. We walked along together for a while.

"That guy Sabaudin who was sitting opposite you," I asked Saxel, "is he the communist?"

"Yes."

In my naiveté, I was surprised. I told my companion so.

"What a funny idea. Why shouldn't a communist visit a countess? Why shouldn't two communists visit a countess? Why not a dozen? Only a reactionary would find it odd."

"Is the countess a communist?"

"On Tuesdays, Thursdays and Saturdays. On Sundays she hears Mass from a heretical priest and other days she invites theosophists and people from other rival sects. Edouard Salton was there yesterday, for instance."

"You can't stand the lady, can you?"

"What drives me crazy is seeing Anglarès in love with her."

"That guy with the potbelly began to get quite nasty."

"I can't think why she invited the bastard at the same time as us."

"Who is he?"

"Some hack writer. Another communist. But he won't accept that we're communists. He doesn't find our principles to be in agreement with his. He's really just a vulgar materialist. In any case, he's a bastard. He spreads a whole lot of lies about us."

"Haven't you joined the Party yet then, Saxel?"

"No, neither has Anglarès. We'd rather wait. He's hoping to get in touch with Moscow directly."

He added: "Don't tell anyone, no one's supposed to know."

"Who would I tell?"

"G., for instance."

"I haven't seen him for months."

"Just as well. There's another narrow-minded guy. He can't see beyond wages and strikes. No use talking to him about mediums and psychic powers: he laughs in your face. There's more serious work to do, he'll tell you."

"That's what he told me when I was learning Arabic."

"Well, I agree with him there. I can't stand Arabs. For one thing, they're all homosexuals."

We were almost at my place. We sat down at a café to have a drink before parting.

"Food wasn't so bad today," said Saxel, referring to the countess again.

"I'm no expert," I admitted, "it seemed OK to me."

"Look, that's probably the point where we differ most from the theosophists and sects like them as well as from the pacifists who tend to be vegetarian as well as from the communists—

they're poor and don't eat well, so they can't judge: we're not puritans, as Jaurès used to say. Talking about Jaurès, it wasn't far from here that he was killed. Funny coincidence."

A beggar loomed up out of the dark armed with postcards. Somber and shaky, he was stammering:

"Take pity on an old worker, take pity on an old worker, I worked for the same people for forty years, sir."

"That was stupid of you," said Saxel, "look what it did for you."

"My two sons were killed in the war, sir."

"That was stupid of them."

"A postcard, sir, just one little postcard."

"Sorry. Never send 'em."

"Come on, old man," a waiter intervened, "are you going to leave these gentlemen alone?"

"Tell me now, did anyone call you over?" Saxel asked him, and he said to the old man:

"Have a drink with us?"

"With pleasure, sir, with pleasure," and he sat down.

The waiter disappeared briefly and returned with the manager.

"Sorry, gentlemen, but we cannot serve this . . ."

"You'll serve him what he asks for," said Saxel.

"No, sir. I'm sorry, but . . ."

"It's a disgrace," shouted Saxel, "he's a human being like the rest of us. He's got a right to have a drink if he's thirsty. You haven't learned a lesson from the Revolution of '89, have you, you with your potbelly?"

A crowd was gathering around us: passing prostitutes, drivers from the nearby taxi stand, sundry nocturnal beings, all took our side. The manager gave in. A glass of red wine was served to the beggar. As he tried to explain something, he waved his arm and knocked it over. They had to bring him another one. He told us all about how he'd been thrown out of the firm where he'd worked for forty years. Saxel tried to inculcate in him a few of the principles of class struggle, but the old man felt nothing but affection for his former boss. Saxel was fed up. He got up. The old man didn't want to leave; he kept beginning his story all over again. Saxel tossed some coins onto the table and we left.

The next day, for no obvious reason, I made my way to the Place de la République. It was not yet twelve. I saw Anglarès, sitting alone at his usual pavement café. He saw me and beckoned me over. I sat down at his table. While I was thinking about what I was going to have, he smiled to himself and gave the lenses of his pince-nez a wipe. Then he looked at me: once again I noticed a funny expression on his face, but he wiped it off immediately, as if he were removing a mask, and he put his pince-nez back on.

"Well, my dear Travy, what do you think of us?"

I thought for a few minutes about how to answer a question like that, but he said again:

"Tell me frankly, what do you think of us?"

He put the question very simply, even pleasantly.

I gaped at him. He said again:

"Saxel did warn me that you weren't very talkative."

He stopped smiling and, without giving me a chance to reply again, he asked a different question:

"Did Dr. Bru give you a ride yesterday?"

"Oh, that was Dr. Bru, was it?"

"Didn't you know him? Weren't you introduced?"

"I didn't catch his name."

"A good guy, isn't he?"

"He might well be. I hardly spoke to him."

Anglarès gave me another long, hard look from behind his pince-nez:

"Was Saxel with you?"

"Yes, he walked back with me."

41

"He doesn't like the countess."

It was not a question; nevertheless I was rather amazed. Anglarès led the conversation in another direction.

"You remember the text that I read the first time you came to my house. But perhaps you've forgotten, so much has happened since . . ."

"I remember very well."

"You've never told me what you thought of Vachol's interpretation of it."

"It was remarkable," I said, "and the text was amazing."

"It was very strange, wasn't it?"

"Very strange," I repeated, and indeed I had sometimes thought back to that performance with some amazement.

"We all possess some powers of prophecy," said Anglarès, "but it isn't given to all of us to discover them. For that to happen, the voice of reason has to fall silent and the intellect must black out, you must let yourself be carried down into the infrapsychic depths, and then you will know the future."

He went on: "It isn't easy. There are few among us who manage it. In these matters, you can leave no stone unturned; that is why we consult clairvoyants and listen to mediums."

He just looked at me.

"We are all, to some extent, mediums and clairvoyants."

He was speaking with great assurance. Feeling impressed, I stared at the statue of the Republic.

"But," he went on, "your scientific background perhaps makes you despise mediums and clairvoyants? Not so, I hope? That would certainly be a mistake on your part. I have the greatest admiration for modern science, and your theories interested me greatly. I've been waiting for a long time for someone like you who could reveal the infrapsychic nature of mathematics," (I had never revealed any such thing) "and who could thereby humanize the most abstract part of modern science. Your presence among us is most certainly a sign, my friend, a great sign."

Convinced as I was that I was a worthless failure, I found it hard to believe such a thing; however, my companion seemed sure of what he was saying. And he had called me "my friend."

Then he said: "I have rarely managed to predict anything as accurately as I did about you. That too must be a sign. You will play a very special role in our group, quite different from the others, I'm sure. Because I can now consider you as part of our group, can't I?"

"Of course," I replied rather uneasily.

His sign, his great sign made me want to laugh and nonetheless impressed me at the same time, for although it seemed funny for such importance to be attributed to me, I could still see that there was something significant in this combination of circumstances. Lacking any redeeming feature as I had been up to then, this new responsibility began to weigh heavily upon me: people might say this or that of me, and what's more, I had to live up to it. Every day brought a fresh commitment. As if to dispel my worries, Anglarès joked about certain over-zealous disciples who would have liked "us to form a secret society with statutes, initiation stunts and secret signs, just like an American fraternity."

"It comes from their theosophist background," he explained to me, "some of them haven't grown out of that old garbage yet."

Just then Vachol appeared: since he was the editor of the *Review of Infrapsychic Research,* Anglarès asked him if my name was on the list of regular contributors; Vachol said it wasn't.

"Well, you can add him to the list now."

He turned to me: "Is that all right?"

"It's a great honor," I replied, laughing.

He smiled very politely and went on:

"Getting back to what I was saying earlier, it is true of course that forming a secret society could be to our advantage once we get involved in revolutionary activity. Once we have formally declared ourselves in favor of the Third International."

"I thought . . ." I began.

"No, not yet. I'll explain more about that to you later. We have an ideological task to perform first. You see, we have to reconcile our theory of psychic phenomena with dialectical materialism."

"And there are some of our number who are not even willing to attempt it," said Vachol.

"Like Saxel," specified Chènevis, who had just looked up with his glaucous eyes, "he doesn't see the point of it."

"Anyway," said Anglarès, "there could be a certain advantage in forming a secret society, if only to stop our meetings being troubled by the Royalist rabble of the far right."

"We're better off without them sticking their dirty noses in our business," said Chènevis, who was one of the main people in favor of having a secret society. "Vis-à-vis communism it may also be necessary," he added. "Within the Party for example would we constitute a special cell or would we each join separately and keep quiet about our group?"

"We'll put that as an item on the agenda of our next general meeting," replied Anglarès, and turning to me, he added: "I hope you'll be there."

I met up again with Odile at Marcel's; she had just spent a month in England with Louis Shard: a month or thereabouts, in any case I hadn't seen her since our meeting with Saxel. I had lunch with Oscar, Odile and S. Since the latter had started work at a garage on the edge of town, he only turned up occasionally and I'm not sure what dealings brought him to Marcel's that day. He greeted me in Arabic, I replied and he started to dig up stories from our soldier days. Oscar and his girlfriend were filling in Odile on every tiny detail of their daily existence during the month she was away. Saxel was mentioned.

Odile knew about him through me; she was quite surprised to hear that he was well known as a racing fan in the Rue du Croissant.

"Sometimes I wonder if it's all right," said Oscar, "are you sure he's not a police spy?"

"Quite sure," I replied.

After a glass of calvados, he left and so did S., to do some business or other. Adèle said to us:

"Well, I'll leave you lovebirds alone."

"What lovebirds?" asked Odile.

"She's a little stupid," I commented.

"As for you," said Adèle, "just because you played a mean trick on me once, it doesn't mean you have to act the tough guy. Isn't that right, Jack?"

"OK, OK!"

"Mr. High-and-Mighty pretends not to be interested in women!"

"You've opened your big trap enough for one day."

"I'll shut up; I've nothing more to say; forget I said anything, bye for now."

She went off saying she just liked a joke. Then Odile and I walked down to the river.

"What happened with your article?" she asked me.

"They published it."

"Are you pleased?"

"Not very."

"Why ever not?"

"I didn't write exactly what I think and now I've gone and become a member of the group!"

"Didn't you want to be?"

"I don't know."

"I thought you thought like them."

"I suppose so."

"Do you blame me for having got you into writing the article?"

"Oh no."

"Not even a little?"

"That's not it. I'm just slightly stunned."

"You're sorry not to be on your own anymore?"

"Perhaps that's it."

"So you do hold it against me?"

"Of course not, but without you I would never have written the paper; I'm not pleased with it."

"So there you are, you do blame me."

"Just think, all because of that, a countess invited me to dinner."

"Quite a society man now!"

"Don't make fun of me. I hated it. There were famous people there, or so they said. I didn't know who they were. They were talking about a lot of stuff I didn't know anything about. In the end I was bored stiff. Saxel was there. He's a great conversationalist."

"And is the countess a communist?"

"I asked Saxel the same question. He said, I can't remember now what he said. But anyway, I don't think so."

"He doesn't really work for *La Veine,* does he?"

"No. He dreamed that up to impress our friends."

"You're sure he doesn't work for the police?"

"Oh, come on, I'm absolutely positive."

"If our friends found out he's telling stories, things might turn nasty."

"True. I'd better warn him. He's so pleased he's got to know them."

Now that I had Odile back, I stopped going to the Place de la République and I only saw Anglarès once before the group's general meeting. I kept in touch with him through Saxel, who often showed up at the Rue Montmartre. Saxel was still nearly as enthusiastic. My friends liked him because he had such a way with words; at the same time they were shocked by him because of his lack of respect for his parents and France. The feeling was mutual; he in turn was bitter when he heard them speaking fondly of their parents and respectfully of France: but he forgave them these outdated sentiments which he considered to be evidence of an inadequate political education, and which didn't surprise him in members of the lumpen-proletariat. However, he was particularly disappointed one day when he heard two of them express remarkably reactionary ideas on the softness of the jury in cases of crimes of passion, ideas that they got from one of Clément Vautel's films.

"Those people are beyond hope," he said to me as he left the café, "you won't catch me coming here again. I don't know how you can have hung around with that crowd for so long."

That made me laugh, and him too. Then we met one of the "crowd," the one called F., who the previous year had stayed in the same boardinghouse as I did and who now lived near the Place Pigalle. This shadowy character walked a little way with us and we exchanged a few banalities.

At that time, one of the theaters on the boulevards was showing a movie whose title I have forgotten but which was supposed to be about hypnotism. We looked absentmindedly at the posters. F. shrugged his shoulders.

"Isn't it a very good movie?" Saxel asked him—out of politeness, presumably—as I can't imagine he would have trusted his judgment.

F. shrugged his shoulders again.

"Well, er . . ."

We asked him to make his views more explicit; he did so, although not without a certain amount of effort. That's when we found out that his sister was a medium, because F. got his categories confused and thought mediums and hypnotists were the same thing; then we learnt something much more interesting, that she was the spirit of Lenin reincarnated, and finally he confided in us ("But swear not to tell anyone, eh!")

that she acted as a "guide" for a small group of spiritualists who also claimed to be revolutionaries. The members of this tiny group were almost all from the working class. Saxel's enthusiasm was kindled afresh. He made F. answer all sorts of questions. Although he was highly surprised at the interest we showed in these people who he thought were a lot of crackpots, he finally promised that he would do "all he could" to get us into the group. Then he left. I don't know what made him keep his word but only two or three days after this meeting, Saxel and I were invited to one of this group's séances; we were supposed to meet with some of the members beforehand in an agreed-upon café in the Rue Nationale. As it turned out, we met only one of them, though he was in fact the most important one: he was a retired customs officer called Mouillard and the meetings where the spirits were summoned took place at his house. This ruddy-faced old gentleman made us welcome, I don't know why; he managed to stop Saxel from holding forth and spent the whole time telling us all about himself, or rather all about the medium—Elisa, he called her—and the history of the group from its origins to the present. I have, of course, forgotten all of this, unfairly perhaps, because I believe that Elisa's life was of some interest. When Mr. Mouillard's story had come to an end, he asked us to follow him, without entering into any discussion of doctrine with my friend Saxel. Mr. Mouillard lived in the Rue Nationale, across a courtyard, in a sort of large studio divided in two by a large red velvet curtain with golden tassels. Mr. Mouillard and his wife seemed to live in the smaller part; in the larger part, the dear lady of the house was looking after about twenty people who were already there when we arrived. On the walls there were a lot of posters, photos, newspaper cuttings, and various documents. While more spiritualists were arriving, Saxel and I stood there feeling rather stupid, because Mr. Mouillard left us to go and say "Good evening, comrade. Good evening, comrade."

At nine o'clock exactly, he went out to bolt a tiny grilled door which separated us from the rest of the world; then he shut the studio door. Curtains were hung across all the windows. The only light left was a red night-light no doubt inherited from the photographer who previously occupied the premises. Everyone sat down elbow to elbow around a very long table. One place was empty. Mr. Mouillard asked for silence, announced that Saxel and I were present, then asked for silence again. The empty place was suddenly taken by the medium who up until now had remained alone behind the big red velvet curtain with golden tassels. After this, there was about a quarter of an hour of complete silence; at about 9:17, Elisa was heard to sigh deeply; and again at 9:19 and 9:23. I was watching the minute hand on Saxel's elegant wristwatch and I could feel he was edgy from the way he was trembling. My right-hand neighbor's elbow and thigh, on the contrary, seemed to be in a state of calm expectancy. The sighs grew more frequent, became a sort of groan. Then Elisa fell silent again. Finally, after about forty minutes' wait, Mr. Mouillard asked in an appropriate tone of voice:

"Spirit of Lenin, are you there?"

"Who are these two new comrades?" answered a voice that sounded almost masculine, doing a passable imitation of a Slav taxi driver.

"They're two comrades from another group who have come here to learn," replied Mr. Mouillard.

"Do they belong to the C.P.?"

Mr. Mouillard, not knowing the answer, kept quiet. People nudged us.

"We don't belong," said Saxel.

"Why not?"

"We're joining any time now."

"You must join the Party, comrade, or you will not be able to listen to my teachings from the dead."

"That would be a pity," muttered Saxel.

"Silence!" reproved the spirit. "Do you have any questions?"

"Of course, of course, we are here to learn."

"One question will be enough for today, comrades. I have no time to waste. Hundreds of other groups are waiting to hear me. Speak, comrades."

"Hm, hm," went Saxel.

"You are intimidated, comrade. The timid cannot make a Revolution. If you are not capable of asking a question, let your friend do it. I'm listening."

My heart missed a beat. Never in the world would I have dared to open my mouth. Saxel took the plunge:

"How can one reconcile dialectical materialism and a belief in the immortality of the soul?"

A suppressed murmur zigzagged its way around the table.

"Silence," said the spirit reprovingly again. "I shall reply to your question, comrade. The spirit of Lenin says: philosophical questions can only be clarified in a classless society once the expropriators have been expropriated. Reflect on that, comrade. Comrade, listen to me. I am going to tell you now about the latest mistake made by the diabolic Jew and black magician, Leon Davidovich Trotsky."

And it started reciting an article out of the *Cahiers du bolchevisme*. After ten minutes it stopped suddenly. Mr. Mouillard got up to put on the lights. Then we were able to see the medium, a pale blonde young girl to whom Madame Mouillard gave a glass of water with sugar in it, as a "tonic" to help her get over her psychic efforts. Mr. Mouillard, looking jovial, came over to us and said encouragingly:

"Come back next Saturday."

The rest of the audience, definitely workers, all respectably dressed, were looking at us suspiciously. We bade good-bye to the assembled company.

"It's frightening," I said to Saxel when we were far enough

away from their den, "isn't it pathetic!"

"That's not the point. They're a lot of simpletons, but we might be able to use them to get our teachings through to the people."

"Do you think so?"

"Yes. All it needs is for me to go to bed with the medium." I indulged in some theatricality which consisted of stopping dead, waiting for the other person to do the same and, when he turned round, looking him straight in the eyes.

"Saxel," I said to him, "I'll never take you seriously again."

"Damn right too. Still, didn't you think she was pretty?"

"Sure I did," I said.

"Did you see those breasts? I shall try and sit beside her next time. Elisa! Elisa the medium! Don't you think she's great?"

"Yes, yes."

"I understand. When you're in love with one woman, the others don't interest you."

"I'm not in love."

"Oh no? What about the attractive young lady for whose sake you put up with all the reactionary talk of those pimps?"

"Get lost, Saxel."

I turned my back on him and left him alone in the night. He stumbled off as if he were drunk.

I saw him the next day. When I arrived, he was telling Anglarès about the events of the previous day.

"And it's an extraordinary place," he was saying, "in the Rue Nationale, right near that amazing Jeanne d'Arc housing project, that 'citadel of revolt,' as *l'Huma* calls it."

And when he saw me:

"I'm sorry about last night."

Anglarès looked at us.

"Don't worry about it," I said.

We shook hands warmly. I sat down.

"We never see you. What's become of you? Were you at the

51

Rue Nationale with Saxel yesterday?"

"He didn't find it very interesting," said Saxel.

"That's not quite true," I said.

"But still, you're not as enthusiastic as he is," said Anglarès.

"Thanks to them, we'll be able to get through to the workers," said Saxel.

"I'm not really up on such things," I said.

"We'll see about that."

Catching sight of Vachol and Chènevis and his wife getting out of a taxi, Anglarès asked us to keep this matter a secret and by the time the others got within earshot we were having a discussion about the next aggressive step that French imperialism would take against the Soviet Union; by *we*, I mean Anglarès and Saxel, with me simply listening, since I knew nothing about international relations. After that I stayed away from the Place de la République for several weeks. The séance at Mr. Mouillard's house had thoroughly depressed me. I got down to work again, because these various distractions had kept me away from my research. Shard had come back from England, and I hardly saw Odile. As for Saxel, he didn't come to the Rue Richer anymore. So I had got back into my old routine when a typed sheet of paper once more dragged me out of my solitude; Anglarès was asking me to come to a general meeting of his group. The following two items were on the agenda: (a) the Mouillard question; (b) membership of the Communist Party. I promised to attend, not so much out of enthusiasm as out of a sense of duty, hoping to serve the cause that I thought I believed in then.

The night before the first meeting, perhaps it was the same day, there was a knock at my door. It was Saxel.

"What's happened to you?" he said.

He glanced at the recurrent sequences that I was in the middle of working out and sat down on my bed.

"What about you?" he asked. "Had enough of these crooks?"

"And you, had enough of spiritualists?"

"I'll say I have." Saxel made a face.

"I see, you'll be against me as well."

"Against you?"

"Yes. I'm very much in favor of an association with the Rue Nationale group."

"It's a free country."

"You've no objection?"

"I haven't thought much about it."

"Have you seen Anglarès?"

"Not since the . . ."

"Well, you'll be seeing him before this evening."

That means it must have been the same day.

"Is that so?"

Saxel smiled:

"He wants to get you on his side. He doesn't want to hear another word about the Rue Nationale group."

I remained silent. He went on:

"It's a weird story. If I told you, you wouldn't believe it. I'll tell you anyway. Well, the countess, you know which countess, the countess had been told, I'm not interested who by, of the existence of Elisa. She wanted to attend a séance. You can imagine she wouldn't want to miss that. I won't go into all her ruses, but in the end I had to take her along. So, there she was at the Rue Nationale. The good part is that she was thrown out. In no time at all. I stayed. And she had to leave. While she was in there, her tires were slashed. You can imagine her face. Anglarès is furious. As the whole affair makes the lady in question look totally stupid, he'd rather keep it quiet. But he'll veto any contact with Mouillard's group. He's indoctrinated all his followers, like Chenevis and Vachol. And I'm sure he'll come and brainwash you before this evening's meeting. Think what you like about it all: you're forewarned. See you later."

Half an hour after he left I did indeed get a note from

Anglarès asking me for dinner.

He wasn't back when I arrived; his wife received me. She asked me to sit down and made conversation. She was a dazzling woman who overpowered me. Seeing that she wouldn't get anything out of me, she easily found an excuse to leave me and disappeared. A volume of *Das Kapital* was lying around on the table; as I was musing surprisedly on the thought of Anglarès's enjoying reading it, he entered without my hearing him.

"Have you never read it?" he asked me from the other end of the room.

"No I haven't," I stuttered.

He had Vincent N. with him. They both looked in a good mood after a drink. I listened admiringly to what they had to say, which I found exceptionally interesting. Madame Anglarès reappeared. We sat down to dinner.

"There was no way of getting rid of Vachol," said Anglarès to his wife. And to me: "Vachol has got into the habit of coming here whenever I have a dinner party, or even when I only have a few friends around; I couldn't make him understand he wasn't wanted."

Then, to my great surprise, N. started to tell a whole series of unpleasant anecdotes about the man, which made Anglarès laugh and his wife snigger. All through dinner their guest singled out each of their friends one after the other to the great satisfaction of our hosts. I laughed at these stories, too, without following them all, but I really couldn't get over it. They got to Saxel, but my fellow guest did not seem to find him an inspiring subject. Anglarès then placed his pince-nez firmly on his nose and, giving me a searching glance, went on the attack:

"Since we're talking about Saxel, I must tell you that it's because of him that I wanted to see you before today's meeting."

"I thought as much," said N. coldly. Anglarès only smiled

54

enigmatically. I was totally overwhelmed by them, and could not utter a word.

"This evening," Anglarès went on, "we are going to discuss an alliance with the communist spiritualist group. Now, these people are of no interest; their medium's revelations are a tissue of stolen ideas and stupidities: the man Mouillard is a cretin and the members are idiots who don't understand a thing. Actually, Travy attended a séance and knows that very well."

The other guest looked at me. I had to say something.

"At least, you don't share Saxel's enthusiasm," said Anglarès to me, getting slightly impatient.

"I didn't know Saxel was enthusiastic," I replied, thinking I'd get out of it that way. The other guy said:

"In any case, Saxel told me himself that after you left Mouillard's, you said 'isn't it pathetic.' "

"I did," I said.

Anglarès took the cue:

"This evening Saxel is going to put the case for this pathetic group. You know him, he's capable of winning over the majority. That would be disastrous. I've got a definitive counterargument up my sleeve but I can't use it. Saxel is a friend of mine. He's a friend of yours. You'll understand that in a discussion of theoretical matters I cannot argue ad hominem. And yet the evidence would be conclusive."

We waited in silence.

"That's why I asked you to come: I wanted you to give your opinion. You see, Saxel's actions in this business are motivated by one thing: he's the medium's lover. He's careful not to tell anyone. Now you can understand why he's acting like he is. It's an act of friendship towards him to get him out of it and thwart his plans. Nine o'clock," he groaned, "we're going to be late. But," and this was addressed to me only, "you won't need to speak against him, of course."

We called for a taxi.

The meeting was to take place in the basement of a café on the Boulevard Beaumarchais. People were sitting around the billiard table. There were loads of people there that I'd seen before, about forty people in all, women and some kids included. I found out later that Belgians, Swiss and Yugoslavs had come specially for the occasion. Left on my own by Anglarès who was besieged by those present, and by Vincent N., who was cornered by someone I didn't know, I was a bit lost in the crowd. They finally decided to get down to business. Everyone crowded around the billiard table two or three deep. Vachol, editor-in-chief of the review, was in the chair. Anglarès withdrew a little out of the light. It was only then that Saxel arrived; there were no more chairs; he sat down on a small table, right at the back. Vachol read out the agenda; no one voiced any objection; we went straight into the Mouillard question. Chènevis read a totally unfavorable report. Saxel protested: "Chènevis has no right to talk about it, he has never attended a séance."

"Correct," replied Chènevis. "In that case I suggest that Travy tell us what he saw and heard when he went to the Rue Nationale."

I looked at Anglarès, who didn't bat an eyelash. The joke was on me and I was sweating profusely. Everyone listened carefully, thinking that I was a genuine witness. So I recounted what I had seen and heard at the Rue Nationale. I was asked what I thought of it; I had to admit that I didn't think much of it. Saxel put forward his arguments:

"It doesn't matter what sort of state the group is in at present. We'll change it and that way we'll be able to get our ideas across to the proletariat."

"Your ideas or ours?" Chènevis asked insolently.

"I said our ideas," replied Saxel, who didn't want the discussion to get bogged down in that particular detail. He went on defending his point of view, he talked and he talked; he really was a good talker, but the audience was skeptical. He got annoyed, went on talking, ended up unable to talk anymore, and resolved to keep quiet. He sat down on his small table. Everyone went quiet to show that they were thinking things over. Something glistened in a dark corner; Anglarès was adjusting his pince-nez.

"I propose that we postpone further discussion of this matter. We need more information. Saxel is the only one of us who is in regular contact with the group in question. We could appoint a subcommittee of three to cooperate with Saxel."

This was unanimously approved. The subcommittee was appointed: it consisted of Anglarès, Vachol and Chènevis. Saxel seemed to be very satisfied with this solution.

All that had taken a long time; so when the second item was reached, someone pointed out that it was already very late to start a discussion about such an important issue, but someone else felt that there was plenty of time and in any case the Yugoslavs had to leave again the next morning. Can't they stay longer? No, they can't. Someone suggests that we have a vote on whether to continue or not. Someone else objects that it's stupid to have a vote, because it's a waste of time. The one in favor of a vote insists. In the end it is decided that we should keep going. A Yugoslav speaks. It's a quarter to twelve. Those who live in the suburbs leave discreetly: this makes Anglarès mad.

"If some of us are not prepared to miss a train for the sake of their principles, then we might as well all go home."

He got up. Chènevis got up. Vachol got up. Everyone got up. The meeting broke up.

The Yugoslavs were not pleased. Anglarès took them aside and had a heart-to-heart with them. The Yugoslavs went off feeling very pleased.

The next day Saxel came and knocked at my door: it was

becoming a habit.

"You see what happened? He fooled me, and you too."

"I'm sorry," I said, "but I had to say what I thought."

"I don't hold it against you. But I've had about all I can take."

"Of what?"

"Of nothing. You saw the subcommittee trick? Fucking red con-tricks stand out a mile. And you heard what Chènevis said? But I didn't fall into that trap. They can go along to the Rue Nationale: they'll see what sort of a welcome they get! I'll arrange a reception committee for them!"

"You're very worked up."

"I've got reason to be. Do you think I'm going to let myself be made a fool of? Anglarès is afraid that I'll take over, don't you realize? He wants to be in charge at the Rue Nationale like he is everywhere else. That's the crux of the matter."

"What about the countess?"

"Ah, yes, the countess. I'm certain now that he means to force her on old Mouillard one of these days. He means to get into bed with her sooner or later. Probably that's the condition she's made, she's mad enough. Wouldn't surprise me in the least."

He grew quiet; a bit calmer now, he explained his position on the proposal to join the Communist Party. On that score he was in agreement with Anglarès: since they hadn't been able to get in direct contact with Moscow, they should all join individually; for there could be no real revolutionary activity outside of the Communist Party. But there was nothing to stop them from meeting to pursue their particular activities, without going as far as forming a sort of secret cell as extremists like Chènevis wanted.

"What about you," he asked me, "what will you do?"

"I'm undecided," I replied, "some of my ideas don't fit very well with materialism, even if it's dialectical materialism."

"Your mathematical ideas, you mean?"

"Yes. I still believe in their intrinsically objective nature. I'm nearer to Plato than to Marx."

"Oh my God," said Saxel absentmindedly.

"But how have you managed to reconcile *your* ideas with . . ."

"I leave that to the Vachols and the Chènevises of this world. Revolutionary action first, theorizing afterwards."

"So what do you recommend?"

"Join!"

Thereupon he left me; we were to see each other again that evening for the crucial meeting.

I left my boardinghouse around five o'clock. In the Place de la Bourse I bought *L'Intransigeant*. I flicked through it as I walked along. I followed the Rue du Faubourg-Montmartre as far as the boulevards. I waited a few moments before I could cross, then I was about to go up the Rue Montmartre. All of this remains quite clear and distinct, as does what was to follow, because whenever anything happened I had developed a facility for imprinting on it my memory. I had committed myself to the world, and, my state of dejection now over, I noticed other people, as any normal man does. Certain periods of my life may have later been eroded in my memory, but that was simply due to human frailty.

So, on the corner of the Rue Montmartre, I met the girl I have called Alice.

"Don't go up there," she said calmly, with no hint of panic in her voice.

I looked at her.

"Should we have a drink?" I suggested.

We crossed the road to go to the Soleil d'Or.

"Well then?"

"Shard . . . Oscar's shot him."

"What's that?"

"Oscar's just shot his brother."

"You're pulling my leg."

"I promise you it's true. They've taken Shard to the hospital and Oscar's been arrested. They've busted F. as well. They're taking the opportunity to round up a few people. Don't go up there. They'll find you soon enough."

"Thanks."

"It's OK; it's OK."

"What can they do to me?"

"You don't know them. They'll find something. Be careful."

"What about Odile?"

"I don't know. She wasn't there."

"Just as well."

"Oh, they'll find her anyway."

"It's a dirty business."

"Don't worry yourself: this sort of thing happens all the time."

"I guess you're right."

"OK. See you later. I gotta go."

"Bye and thanks again."

"Don't worry about it, eh, it doesn't help."

We said good-bye. I watched her ass vanish into the distance. It vanished.

I was left looking at two beers, untouched and gone flat. After a few twilight moments, I started to think about the matters that were coming up at that evening's meeting. I wondered if I was going to join the Communist Party, and to what extent I was really a communist, and to what extent the others were really communists, and what advantages there would be in the founding of a secret society.

And where is Odile? What is she doing? Rotten egotist thinking only of yourself. Perhaps they had put her in jail? But why should they have put her in jail? That's a ridiculous thought. She must be at the hospital. Shard may be dead. If Oscar's aim was good, Shard must be dead now.

Odile?

I paid for my two beers and decided to pass by her place. The shortest way was via the Rue Montmartre. So I went down the Rue Montmartre and steeled myself to go as far as Rue Richer. With pounding heart and dry mouth, I did, however, take the precaution of walking on the other side of the road. Marcel's was closed. In front of the door a small crowd was talking about the shootings. I went by without looking around. If anyone had so much as touched me with their little finger, I would have fainted. I kept going, but I was getting more and more worried. I went up the Rue du Faubourg-Poissonnière as far as the Rue du Delta. Carried along by my anxiety, I walked right past the hotel without stopping; I turned back at the Square d'Anvers. I walked past the hotel a second time. The third time I went in. Odile wasn't there. Her landlady didn't look at me at all suspiciously: there was nothing strange about her not being there. I left. It was around eight o'clock. Crowds were thronging the boulevard. I sat down on a bench, overwhelmed by a sense of my own helplessness; crowds of people rushed past me. I watched them to take my mind off everything. Every so often I gave some vague thought to the important question of joining the Communist Party, and the meeting that was to take place that same evening. Odile must be at the hospital of course. In a little café like Marcel's a couple of revolver shots must have made a real racket. The noise was reverberating in my ears. I was hungry. I went into the first restaurant I found and ate as much as I could. Then I felt I needed a brandy. I didn't feel I could face the meeting in the Boulevard Beaumarchais; I would have gone home if I hadn't been afraid there might be a policeman waiting for me. And yet the murder had nothing to do with me; it was that idiot Alice who had scared me.

So I went to see a funny movie. As I went home around midnight I passed by Odile's hotel again; no one could tell me anything much. On my way home Marcel's was still closed. I bought a packet of sleeping pills in an all-night drugstore. In my hotel nothing special awaited me.

Next morning, when I woke up about eleven o'clock, I phoned; they had begun to sound suspicious. My landlord mentioned yesterday's incident as well. I went out. At the top of the Stock Exchange steps there was the usual din. I bought a copy of *Paris-Midi*; Shard had died. No mention of Odile. There was an article calling for Paris to be cleaned up and for the thugs who messed around with guns to be given harsh sentences. No mention of Odile. I went by Odile's hotel again and got a bad reception. That evening in the papers I learned that S., my army friend who was working in a garage, had been arrested; they were cleaning up.

The second day was empty, miserable, full of grief. The weighty problems of dialectics and of the unconscious had all gone from my mind; I didn't even think of filling the void by going to the Place de la République, I had forgotten about Saxel, Anglarès and the others. That day I think I even cried.

On the third day, I received a visit from two gentlemen who showed me a piece of paper and said:

"We've come to see if we can find anything of interest."

They started going through my papers. One of them came upon my recurrent sequences.

"What's all this?"

"Calculations."

"What sort of calculations?"

"Just calculations. I'm a mathematician."

He shrugged his shoulders.

"Are you a student?" the other one asks me.

"Yes."

"What are you doing with that bunch?"

"What bunch?"

"Don't pretend you don't know."

It is his turn to shrug his shoulders.

"A good kid got mixed up with a bad crowd," he mutters.

These gentlemen were beginning to annoy me; they sounded as if they were going to give me a lecture. On the spur of the moment, I decided to ask them a question:

"Excuse me, but just what is happening?"

They went on rifling through my papers.

"So we're a communist as well, are we?" exclaimed number two.

Was I or wasn't I? Should I say yes out of bravado, or no out of truthfulness? I said nothing. Number one flicked through my collection of the *Review of Infrapsychic Research.* He looked pained. The other glanced through them as well.

"This is serious!" he said and shrugged his shoulders.

For Christ's sake, all they could do was shrug their shoulders.

"What right have you got . . ." I began to say.

"Don't try your clever stuff on us, sir," number two interrupted.

I don't like how he calls me sir; he doesn't think I'm a real criminal. I sit on the edge of my bed and keep quiet. They go on rummaging around. Finally, number two says to me:

"We'll take a closer look at your pieces of paper. Don't worry, we'll let you know when we've finished with them."

They piled up my papers and reviews and picked them up. They left, number one saying nothing and number two turning to say:

"You needn't worry, nothing much will happen. Your family'll bail you out."

He closed the door behind him. He really annoyed me! I was knocked flat, both by his parting thrust and because I didn't know what had happened to Odile. It occurred to me at that moment that my fellow revolutionaries of the unconscious had let me down royally, as we used to say in those days. And then of course there was a knock on the door. It was Vincent N.

"Saxel asked me to come," he said, having a quick look around the room and at me.

"Oh yeah?" I asked.

"He didn't come himself because he was afraid of trouble."

I started to laugh.

"We wondered what had happened to you," Vincent N. went on.

It was my turn to shrug my shoulders.

"Two cops came and went through my stuff," I said, "and they've left with all my papers."

"We'll have to get you out of it," said N.

"I wonder how."

It was his turn to laugh.

"That's easy. The countess can fix it."

"Can she?"

"Friends at the top."

"I can't phone her though."

"No, you can't, but Anglarès can. Any time he's in trouble, she gets him out of it. I mean it, come to the Place de la République and explain everything to Anglarès."

So I explained everything to Anglarès as he sat behind his aperitif. He made a face.

"It's going to be difficult."

"Why on earth?" Vincent N. asked.

"We've already asked her so many favors."

"But it's important this time."

"Took all your papers, did they?" Anglarès asked me.

"Yes and even some copies of the *Review* and your circular and your pamphlets," I volunteered innocently.

Anglarès shuddered.

"We had better do something fast," he exclaimed, shaking his head of hair and rushing downstairs to the phone.

"What a character," Vincent N. said trying not to laugh, "you said just the right thing to him. Still, I like him."

I was in no condition to try and make sense of these cryptic words, for what had become of Odile? What sort of trouble must she be in? It was my turn to rush down to the phone. Through the window of the telephone booth I saw Anglarès smiling and bowing as he held the receiver in his hand. I opened the door.

"What's the matter?" he asked furiously and put his hand over the receiver quickly.

"I'm sorry, but couldn't the countess do something for Shard's friend, Mademoiselle Odile Clarion?"

"I suppose so," he said gruffly.

With that promise I left him to bow and scrape and went back up. A few minutes later he reappeared.

"She's going to help you," he said, "she'll give you a call this afternoon to let you know the outcome."

Sure enough, at about ten in the evening came the phone call that I had waited for all day. The lady informed me that she had arranged everything, my papers would be given back immediately, no one would bother me again; as for the other person, I was not to worry, she was being taken care of also. The countess took the opportunity of inviting me to dinner.

The next day I was called before a magistrate. I went to Odile's hotel first of all; they told me she'd left but no one knew where she was; I left, stuttering an excuse, gripped by anxiety and fear. I walked very quickly from the Rue du Delta to the Palais de Justice. Here I was before the magistrate. I recognized him immediately; I had forgotten his name but I remembered him as soon as I saw him: he used to be a friend of the family who came to see my parents. I pretended not to recognize him. He asked me to sit down in a very courteous tone in which I thought I detected a hint of irony. I knew beforehand what he was going to say. He began:

"I see, my dear fellow, that heaven and earth are moved

when you are inconvenienced by the course of justice. I congratulate you for managing to combine such powerful patrons with such radical opinions. In any case, your patrons need not have worried because everything points to your innocence, your complete innocence, I may say."

He gave me a canny look.

"As for your papers, journals and other documents, please excuse the overzealous conduct of a police officer who has had far less of an education than you. They will be returned immediately; you can get them back from the Clerk's Office. I'm quite pleased with the way things have turned out because it has given me a reliable source of information about the strange sect to which I believe you belong. But I might tell you that what interested me most were your personal papers. I had to look through them, that's my job, and you'll understand how interested I was when I tell you that I'm something of an amateur mathematician too. You won't be too surprised because you're an admirer of Fermat, who was a magistrate, although of course I am not comparing myself with that famous and obscure genius. In the old days I spent long hours trying to prove his famous theorem but in the end I realized it was futile. I have to say, however, I have to say that I think his theorem is either right or wrong, I'm not a follower of Brouwer. And what about you, my dear sir, are you a believer in the validity of the law of the excluded middle?"

Should I get into a discussion with this bourgeois? Guys like me, communists-to-be, shouldn't make conversation with a magistrate; anyway he had insinuated that I was only an amateur mathematician because he said "too."

"I've just asked you a question, my dear young sir. As it has nothing to do with either Shard's murder or his brother's little dealings, I assure you that you can answer without compromising yourself."

"First of all, sir, please don't call me 'my dear young sir.' "

"I'm sure you'd be even more offended if I called you 'my dear child,' and yet I knew you as a child."

"You didn't know me as a child or an adult."

"I don't quite understand what you're saying. In any case, I'll just call you 'sir' if you prefer."

"Thank you."

"Now we know where we stand. To get back to the law of the excluded middle. What do you think about it?"

Did he really think that I was only an amateur? Maybe that's not what he meant by his "too." Since I didn't answer, he went on:

"I'm glad you're not under suspicion, because I would have had to sweat blood and water to get anything out of you! Something I would have wanted to get straight for instance would have been the following: do you hang out with those people because you find them exotic?"

"I can't stand anything exotic."

"Of course, that is what I would expect from a mathematician."

"I adore anything exotic."

"And that's what I would expect from you."

"And every single thing that you have said has been just what I would have expected from a magistrate who patted me on the head as a child."

"Well, I can't agree with you there. Just by the way, you realize that you now admit that I knew you as a child. If this were a 'real' hearing, that is if we were not speaking as 'friends,' that would be a mark against you. In any case, I don't think that every single thing I said et cetera. For instance, I haven't tried to lecture you about your recent adventure."

"Thanks for that."

"I haven't tried to bring up the pain it caused your father when he learned that you were involved in what we call an underworld killing."

"He must have been delighted."

"On the contrary, I've tried to keep our conversation at an objective level, that of pure mathematics."

"But why don't you just let me go instead of making conversation with me, instead of tormenting me? Can't you see that I don't enjoy your questions? What's the purpose of them all? You've got the advantage of being in a position of authority over me. You're inflicting petty torture on me because it's in your power to do that but nothing else. Don't you realize that it's torture for me to have to make conversation with a magistrate, Mr. Magistrate? Of course you realize very well and that's why you insist on trying to talk about math with me. As if I'd be interested in talking about math to a magistrate."

"How funny! You're the one who is giving me a lecture! Do you really think I'm a sadist? I didn't know that there was any harm in discussing mathematics with an expert; I don't often have the chance. In any case, I wouldn't want to prolong a session that you find so painful. You can go now."

I got up.

"Oh, one more thing. Your powerful patrons are also concerned about the fate of Mademoiselle Clarion. Please note: I didn't say 'that Clarion girl.' She's someone who is from a very good family and her situation seems to me to be a little like your own. Such coincidences are quite common in daily life; you must know this as well as I do. In any case, let me reassure you on that score: her name will not be mentioned any more than yours will, she won't have any trouble, any more than you will. Don't you think it's good of us?"

"Why should I have any trouble? I'm innocent, aren't I? And if Mademoiselle Clarion didn't come from a very good family, as you put it, if she were some unfortunate woman off the streets, you'd be less tolerant towards her."

"You see, you see! You're the one who's giving me a lecture again! Ah, these young people!"

I finally escaped from the clutches of this well-meaning torturer. When I got home laden with my papers, I found a letter from Odile, and Saxel waiting for me in person. He was reading *L'Humanité,* which didn't seem to please the landlord. We went up to my room.

"So you got your papers back?"

"No problem," I replied.

Odile's note was to ask me to meet her that evening, but she didn't say anything about herself. I put her letter in my pocket. I cut some string and undid journals and manuscripts.

"Have you heard from . . .?"

"She's not under suspicion either."

"Have you said thank you?"

"Oh dear, I didn't think of it. She's invited me to dinner."

"I'll see you there."

"That's good. So I should thank her, should I?"

"It's the usual thing."

"I'll send her a postcard with 'thank you' on it."

"Good idea. She'll be pleased as long as it's a nice picture."

"I'll choose one at random."

"That's the best idea."

"So I should thank you and Anglarès as well."

"Don't worry. Tell me about it: how was it?"

"I got landed with a real pain: a magistrate who's interested in math and who knew me as a child!"

"What a strange coincidence."

"He wanted to make conversation with me and he tried to get me talking about the proof of Fermat's theorem, Brouwer, and the law of the excluded middle but I didn't play ball."

"Good for you. What was he talking about though?"

"Of course, it's something that might interest you. It's about whether there are mathematical propositions which are neither true nor false."

"I don't follow you."

"To put it another way: are there some propositions that one can never prove or disprove? Some people say there are; some people even think that there might be some propositions that you could prove that you could never prove true or false. Between true and false the middle is not excluded."

"All that is fascinating stuff. I find it very dialectical. Don't you?"

"To a realist like me there can only be true or false propositions."

"No two ways about it, Travy, I'm afraid you haven't got the makings of a real revolutionary."

"You can explain to me one of these days what dialectics is. G. never managed to."

"Don't look down on G. In the last analysis, I think he's right. You have to put the revolution first! The revolutionary struggle: workers' claims, strikes, propaganda."

"You seem to have changed your mind on these matters."

"My ideas have evolved. I want to join forces with the proletariat and become a militant."

"And does Anglarès want to become a militant too?"

"Yes, he does."

"You're beginning to impress me."

"Didn't we impress you before?"

"Have you seen the Rue Nationale people again?"

"People? Comrades, you mean. Of course I've seen them again."

"Do they still believe in the spirit of Lenin?"

"Don't make fun of them. They're very genuine. Of course if the Party knew what they're doing, they'd be excluded immediately. And the Party would be right."

"I can't understand why you're interested in that sect."

"It shouldn't be hard to understand."

He had replied roughly; but he went on:

"Am I wrong to love that woman?"

"For one thing I never said or implied that you were wrong and for another you seem to think I know who you're talking about."

"Do you think I don't know Anglarès told you I was Elisa's lover!"

I thought it was better to keep quiet rather than sound too naive.

During dinner Saxel tried to explain to me what dialectics were but he didn't manage to formulate his ideas on the subject clearly. I left him to go and meet Odile. She was waiting for me in a café near the Gare de Lyon. She seemed the same as ever. I was about to express my surprise but she didn't give me a chance, and before I found out anything about her I was telling her all that had happened to me during the last four days. I went over the events in detail and I even told her about the law of the excluded middle because it seemed to interest her. I finally exhausted all my pitiful news. I didn't like to ask her anything. Lots of people were coming and going, sitting down and standing up, drinking and reading, all sorts of people. I watched them coming and going, sitting down and standing up. Then she said to me:

"I'm going."

"You're going?"

"I'm leaving. I meant to say I'm leaving."

Then she went on:

"What else can I do, what'll become of me? Go out to work? I don't think I'm up to it. Earn a living like the other girls? Being on the streets is too sordid. I couldn't face it. So I'm leaving."

"But where will you go? You can't just get up and leave. Where would you go?"

"You won't like what I'm going to say: I'm going home to my parents in the provinces. They'll take me back: they've forgiven me."

"It sounds terrible."

"Summer's coming. I'll be in the country. It's as if I was going on holiday. Don't you think?"

"I think it's horrible."

"What else can I do? They'll leave me alone. I know they will. I'll have no regrets. I don't have anything to miss. What sort of life have I had up to now? You know very well. So? The only thing I'll miss is you because you've been a good friend. Nothing else means anything. I'll send you postcards to let you know if I'm still alive. Not long, because I'm not good at writing."

"Well I wasn't expecting this," I said, which made her laugh at me.

I looked chastened:

"Isn't there really anything I could do for you?"

"What?"

I couldn't think of anything.

"Well, there you are, I guess the best thing is just to go. Bye."

"What about my train, I don't want to miss my train. I've reserved a seat."

"Shall I come with you?"

"As long as you don't get all upset."

I went with her to the lockers. I carried her suitcase. I bought her some magazines, some fruit, at her suggestion. There weren't many passengers on the night train. I hired some pillows for her as well. I settled her in.

"Look, I'm traveling second class," she said, "it'll look better when I get there. Small-town mentality!"

"I can't get over you leaving: just like that."

"Whatever you do, don't get out your hanky when the train leaves."

"Don't worry. But don't you think we could work things out some other way?"

"It's a little late to think about that now."

"You're right. It's a little late. But even so."

"Don't get upset about it."

"Even so."

"Come on, you're not the sort of person who gets upset."

"Of course not. There, they're starting to yell out."

"Get down or you'll come with me."

I got down.

"So you'll write?"

"I promise."

"I forgot to tell you: I'm going to move. The landlord's not very pleased with me. I can't stand him. I'm going somewhere else."

The whistle blew.

"Write to me poste restante at the Rue Monge post office."

"You're going to live near there?"

"I don't know. It'll give me a walk anyway. Except I'll be all alone."

The train started off.

"So, bye then."

"Good-bye, Odile. Don't forget: poste restante, Rue Monge."

"Bye-bye."

Her head disappeared. I turned around and walked back alongside the train which was gathering speed to my right until I got to the red light. I went out of the station and as if to make a fresh start I decided to leave that same evening. But when I got back I was so exhausted that I thought it better to stay there one more night and to move the next day. I woke up out of a deep sleep and packed my bags. The landlord loathed the sight of me ever since I had pulled strings to get myself out of a tight spot. He thought it was unfair.

I moved to a boardinghouse in the Faubourg Saint-Martin. This meant that I was near the Place de la République and so I went to have a drink there regularly and went to Anglarès's home several times a week. The evening's program hardly varied. We started with a well-prepared meal, as Anglarès set great store by his food; he claimed that game, dishes cooked in sauce, mature cheeses and strong wines were conducive to the development of one's psychic faculties and he did not stint himself on anything that could contribute to the development of his own faculties in this respect. After dinner the "experiments" began—for they brazenly claimed to be part of the experimental sciences, mentioning the names of Claude Bernard, Charcot and Dr. Encausse, better known by his Latin name. These experiments had their starting point either in games to whose rules Anglarès or occasionally one of his acolytes dreamt up variations, in order to confer on them a "psychic" significance, or else in divinations, which Anglarès modified according to the dictates of his unconscious. The aim of these experiments, which varied frequently because Anglarès changed his mood frequently, were less to predict the future than to highlight associations of what the un-initiated would call strange, bizarre, eccentric ideas or facts, or coincidences to which were attributed an amazing or preter-natural quality. In any case they put Anglarès's vocation beyond a doubt and provided "objective" proof for it, the subjective part being taken care of by his hangers-on. In this way it was also possible to accord varying degrees of recogni-tion to the brilliant ideas of his followers depending on how fond Anglarès was of them, or how keen he was to secure their loyalty. A defector from Salton's group had sworn allegiance after he had been persuaded that the stamp of election could be seen upon his whole life, but Anglarès had a good laugh about it afterwards; in private he often took it upon himself to augur both ill and well. On the other hand, if he found an individual uninteresting or he didn't like the look of him, he categorically refused him the honors of a "coincidence."

These then were the "games" they played until it was time for the previous day's predictions, which as I've already described brought the séance to a close. A detailed account of these activities provided the experimental part of the *Review of Infrapsychic Research* and there was thus no trouble in finding material for it. But the question of joining the communists was now disturbing this routine. Meetings took precedence over mediums and the Chinese question over the science of dreams. The new converts were filled with extreme ardor. When Vachol got into contact with real workers, he nearly died of ecstasy. Chènevis, true to form, secretly hoped to pull a few strings and did not give up hope of seeing *L'Humanité* giving over the first floor of its premises to the psychic problems of the masses and to the unpredictable manifestations of the proletarian unconscious. Saxel, on the other hand, was moving towards a more orthodox position, so much so that he was able to convince his mistress that she was not actually the spirit of Lenin reincarnated, for the very good reason that spirits do not "return" and that "superstition" is the "morphine of the workers," as he metaphorically said. So this attractive young lady stopped obfuscating the class consciousness of the inhabitants of the Rue Nationale and would come and drink an aperitif at the same table as Anglarès, who would bow low when she arrived. As for Mouillard's group, it went to the dogs, and was never heard of again. There were still some people who refused to join the C.P. for varying reasons, but their position was becoming very difficult. Vincent did not hide his dislike of Moscow and got attacked by the purists who talked Ulyanov at him all the time. He stuck to his guns. As far as I was concerned though, if I sang the 'International' at meetings and clapped wildly at the showing of the *Battleship Potemkin,* one of their films, I nevertheless hesitated to become a convert. Apart from that they left me in peace; the events in which I had just been involved meant that I was treated indulgently, at least for the time being.

This first wave of enthusiasm was interrupted by the

summer. Some people went to the sea, others to the country. Anglarès went off to ferment in a dungeon in Touraine in the hope of seeing a few ghosts. Only Vincent and I stayed in Paris. He thought of me as an individualist, and I respected his independent spirit. All of this meant that we got friendly at about the time I got the letter for which I had been waiting for over two months, and shortly after that our curiosity led us to be swept along one evening by a threatening crowd. There was a demonstration for two innocent men who had been condemned to death. It began at the bottom of the Champs-Elysées. We followed the procession as it went up the Champs-Elysées singing the International and chanting slogans and injunctions. There was no sign of the cops; respectable citizens on café terraces beat an undignified retreat. The triumphant procession got as far as the Etoile, the only interruption being a revolver shot fired from Fouquet's. Projectiles were thrown at that den of reactionaries; some women started shouting. It was left at that. When we got to the Arc de Triomphe, the flame had already been put out; half a dozen comrades had cornered a lone policeman who attempted to joke and make them believe that he was on the right side. The demonstrators split up, some to the left and others to the right. We went up the Avenue des Ternes. Most of the cafés were shut. It was then that I caught sight of G. with Sabaudin, who I'd met at the countess's house.

"Things were getting hot on Boulevard Sébastopol," said G. "They've put up barricades."

"You gonna go there?" asked Vincent.

"We're trying to find a taxi," replied Sabaudin. "Barricades! What a fantastic day this is!"

We found a taxi on the Avenue de Villiers. It set off quickly for Place Clichy. We were chattering excitedly about this nighttime takeover of the Champs-Elysées. The police had occupied Place Clichy. The taxi doubled back to Rue Richer.

The driver reveals to us that he is a Party member; he maintains that people have been killed, but he doesn't say where he gets his information from. At any rate he avoids the roadblocks, dodging about and cutting down side streets. We end up at the Rue Saint-Denis. We get out. The boulevards are swarming with police. There are people pretending to have a quiet walk; but not a single car. Everything seems calm. On Boulevard Sébastopol there are a lot more people but it's all over. We just walk by, but the police search you or question you every fifty yards. We look at the smashed shop windows, the shoe boxes which litter the ground, the smashed up grills from around the trees, the lone barricade. When there are no cops nearby, we grunt to show our approval. We go down the boulevard towards the Seine. Policemen, onlookers, and ex-demonstrators mingle. It all seems very confused to me. Up at the Halles the cops have disappeared. A crowd gathers immediately to hear contradictory tales of heroism. The tale of the unfinished barricade rekindles hope in the hearts of the latecomers. The cops put in a sudden appearance and run towards the gathering. We move rapidly towards the Halles. Up two or three deserted streets we come across a new mob where stories are flying about. And again the cops arrive. This time I see them close up. They look as if they mean business. One guy falls to the ground near me, clobbered on the head. I roll on the ground, I don't quite know why. I get up to hear unpleasant sounds being shouted in my ear. I stride out in a dignified fashion and catch up with G. Vincent N. and Sabaudin have disappeared. I turn round in time to see them being ignominiously carted off: I am indignant. G. says to me:

"Don't worry, they'll let them go tomorrow morning."

We continue to retreat. It's business as usual at the Rue de Rivoli. We reach the Seine.

"I'd better go home now."

"Where do you live?"

"Faubourg Saint-Martin."

"Wait for things to calm down. Come back with me. I live on Avenue du Maine. I'm going back. There's nothing else we can do."

I went with him, answering his questions: he interrogated me closely about Anglarès and his disciples.

"And you haven't joined up?"

"No," I replied.

"Why not?"

What answer could I give that he would understand? I could feel that he was ready to try and indoctrinate me, which annoyed me.

"Well?" he asked.

All I could say was: "I don't know, I'm just not convinced."

"After an evening like that, you're not convinced?"

"I found it a moving experience," I said.

"What do you mean, 'moving'? What a funny idea to call it 'moving'! Do you realize it's the first time a barricade has been put up in Paris since the Commune? That's what's important: the proletariat of Paris got some experience of street-fighting."

And all the way to his home in Rue Saint-Jacques he explained the techniques of street-fighting. As he climbed up his stairs he must really have pitied me.

When Anglarès got back from his castle, he was keen to hear what we had seen of the demonstrations and did not tire of giving us a list of signs which showed that certain details of his life coincided with some of the events of the riots, thereby managing to convince us that the latter was the result of the former. All of this seemed to him to be another good reason for militating within the Communist Party, although disillusionment was to set in. Chènevis was thrown out of *L'Humanité* when they heard him (to their great amazement) maintaining (what gall!) that the Revolution should find inspiration in such non-rational states as dream, drunkenness and certain forms of madness. It was a big scandal and Saxel said that Chènevis was in the wrong. Then Vachol made an equally bad blunder by stating that it was every worker's duty to assault every priest that he came across: he was taken for an agent provocateur, or at least for a troublemaker. Saxel said that Vachol was in the wrong. Then Anglarès soon got tired of going to his cell, a street cell where he only met concierges and café owners who were distrustful of the wide black ribbon on which his pince-nez hung, his shoulder-length hair and his way of dressing, which was half-Rosicrucian salon and half-cocktail era. And these people were so common that they did not even succumb to his withering look. So when they wanted to get him to bone up on the state of the European economy to explain it to them, he decided he'd had enough. Just when I got Odile's second letter, Anglarès and his eleven or thirteen close friends who had joined the Party less than six months previously were leaving it, disappointed and despairing of a revolution whose future was in the hands of such thugs as the hardline communists.

However, their withdrawal caused a schism: Saxel and two or three others stayed loyal to Moscow. They still came for a drink sometimes, they visited Anglarès sometimes, but the more orthodox disciples only tolerated them in deference to their former friendship, and whereas two months before they had almost branded as traitors anyone who didn't join the C.P., now they took the same line with those who wouldn't leave it. Vincent, on the other hand, surprised me because he didn't seem pleased with the new turn of events; he was afraid that the "secret society" faction would get the upper hand. In any case, some were agitating about one thing, others about another; discussions, disputes and blows below the belt became increasingly common; points were debated with opposing sects, and manifestos were signed with allied groups; but no one knew what to do. They were waiting for

Anglarès to launch the latest bandwagon so that they could all climb aboard to thunderous applause; for the time being he was unusually cautious. He confined himself to introducing us to new games; we dabbled in chance, we explored the infra-conscious and we practiced prediction by numbers according to rules which were the product of pure fantasy, as I have related elsewhere. I dabbled, explored, practiced; prediction by numbers was partly my doing; I explained mathematical games to Anglarès and even if he didn't understand them, he used them to absolutely astonishing metaphysical effect. I witnessed with surprise and curiosity all these comings and goings that went under the name of political activity. True, they continued to curse bourgeois society and to yearn for a new social order: but for the time being the main activity seemed to consist in not buying *L'Humanité* anymore. Since I had never done so . . .

Saxel, whom I liked, was no longer around. Rallies, meetings of his branch or section, and reading *Das Kapital* took up his every waking moment. Vincent N. became my best friend. The rigor of his judgment surprised me so much that I sometimes wondered what he was doing in our group; Anglarès both liked and disliked his independent approach; he got annoyed with him especially when he deliberately broke up an "experiment" that was taking place, because Vincent would not infrequently protest about what he called the "inadequate nature" of certain procedures and would refuse to take part. I learned a lot from him, a lot: a lot, that is, relative to the area in which we were all floundering around.

Having fallen there unwittingly, I gathered a bit of moss, a harmless, bewildered stone. Vincent took it on himself to make me more aware of what was around me, at least at that level; he told me the histories of the sects and the lives of the individuals, the alliances and feuds, the realignments and splits, he filled me in on a host of different points of view, on

80

systems colliding, theories breaking up, arguments bubbling over, and proliferating *isms,* budding and fissiparous, like minute vibrions. When I had mastered all these details, I realized that it had not really got me anywhere at all.

At the same time, I began to get worried about the real value of my research, though only from time to time, for I preferred to press on with it, without hesitating. And I would say to myself:

"If I loved her it would be so simple. What wouldn't one do for a woman that one loves? If I loved her, I'd go and fetch her and bring her back here. What would we live on? I might even work if I loved her. Yes, that's it, I would go and fetch her and maybe we would go off together, for she might not want to come back here, we'd go to Spain or Morocco and I might even meet that Arab again who stood steadfastly gazing at the world, contemplating whatever it was on the road which goes from Bou Jeloud to Bab Fetouh skirting the walls of the town. But how could we go away together? Oh, if I loved her, no doubt I would find some way of leaving this old city where we first met each other."

But that's the problem, it's very difficult to do someone a favor, especially a woman, to help her or rescue her. Everyone immediately thinks you're in love with her and I didn't want anyone to think that: or even worse that I was a sentimental fool. I didn't know what to do. Sometimes I suddenly felt as though I had to do something, but I didn't get beyond that first impulse and I just went on feeling sorry for her and missing her without managing to work out anything definite. What's more, these ideas did not come to me all that often. She lived on for me only in my memory because I didn't see anyone who had known her; as they had all been dispersed by the revolver shot that killed their most illustrious member in the Rue Richer one day in June, she lived on only in memory and I never went to the places where we used to go together. Our friendship had

had six months of separation now, six months, or more correctly one hundred and forty-six days, I counted: I could still count correctly.

Days and memory: some days condense events as if to make them easier to remember; so it was on the twelfth of December of that year. My washbasin was blocked because the day before I had drunk more than I could take. Emerging out of the stupefied spiral of drunkenness, I ran a trembling hand over my drawn face, and hesitated to use my razor. It was getting late. There was a knock from the cleaner who wanted to do my room. I glanced blankly at a sheet of paper which was lying on my table: given two simple regular stems with unique alternating branches, find the number of their points of intersection as a function of the twelve quantities on which their symbolic representation depends in relation to two coordinate axes: the fact that six quantities were necessary, in order to represent such a geometric figure unambiguously, was something that I claimed as my own discovery: actually it was just an observation from which I could deduce nothing so far. I picked up an exercise book; it contained calculations of a new class of numbers that I believed I had invented, numbers whose two elements formed the extreme terms of a double inequation: with regard to the three operations other than addition they manifested extremely curious properties that I couldn't quite figure out; research on what I called the induction of infinite sequences and Parseval's integrals, on what I defined as right addition and left addition with complex numbers and the importance of these operations for combinatorial topology. Numbers, numbers, numbers. There was a knock on the door from the chambermaid who wanted to make my bed. I decided to go to the barber's for a shave and treat my face to a warm towel. I began to feel more like myself again. After a big cup of black coffee and a few paces back and forth down the axis of a figure 8, I felt absolutely fine. I wonder now what on earth I was thinking of all that time. Around mid-day I got within sight of the café in the Place de la République. I saw Anglarès and Vachol and two other characters I didn't know. There was nothing surprising about seeing two new faces, Anglarès loved anyone new: it was enough for some individual to cross the path of his life at what he thought was an unusual angle for Anglarès to make him one of his disciples immediately even if the person concerned had none of the normal qualifications for membership of the group; that had been the case with me. Since Anglarès's enthusiasm waned as quickly as it waxed, the neophyte would disappear, sometimes quietly, often noisily. It gave rise to insulting letters, exclusions and curses, in brief, it was just like in real life.

One of the two characters was none other than Vladislav, a painter whom Saxel had often pointed out to me at Mont-parnasse and whose talent was much admired in the Place de la République, bũt from afar, for up until now he had always rejected any approach by Anglarès. As for the other one, I nearly choked when I heard someone say his name: Edouard Salton. I gaped at that well-known bastard, a cop, a queer, a good-for-nothing. Anglarès and he were chatting in a friendly fashion; more precisely they made occasional friendly com-ments to each other while listening to Vladislav the painter. The latter was recounting how he had practiced necrophilia on a stormy day in Brittany and how he could only paint barefoot while sniffing at a handkerchief soaked in absinth and how in the country after the summer rains he sat down in warm mud to get back in contact with mother nature and how he ate raw meat tenderized à la Attila the Hun, which made it absolutely delicious. Listening to him, no one could doubt he was a painter of genius. His peroration was interrupted by the arrival of Chènevis; he had important news to tell us: thanks to his conciliatory skills we could count on the support of the dissident socio-Buddhist group which consisted of three people, but good guys. Everyone applauded this including me, although I didn't know what it was all about. Thereupon Chènevis, Vachol, Salton and Vladislav went off to have lunch with the three D.S.B. concerned so as to draw up a definitive treaty of alliance, which was guaranteed to last for the rest of the year. I stayed alone with the Master, Anglarès I mean, who asked me with a smile:

"You must have been very surprised to find Edouard Salton here?"

"Somewhat," I admitted.

"You'll forgive me for not having told you what was going on, but you'll find out why: some plans need to hatch in the dark if they're to come to anything."

"Of course."

"There are some things that can't be done collectively. You have to put your faith in me."

"Naturally."

"Have you got a moment? I'll explain to you what we're up to."

"Please do."

"Well, here you are. My intention is to bring under our wing all the separate sects and scattered groups: those of course that are close, or pretty close, to us, that's why you just saw Salton here. I was somewhat reluctant to contact him but one cannot deny that his ideas and ours have something in common. And maybe I judged him a bit too harshly. In any case, with him comes Vladislav, and Vladislav is a great advantage: you realize how well-known he is. We'll make him honorary president and we'll be able to unite under his name. . . . In a way that we could not under mine," he added with a smile.

He went on: "Of course, even if the realignment does not take effect, it'll give us the chance to spread our ideas and perhaps to attract to our cause a few lost souls who didn't know about us. What do you think?"

"Indeed," I said, "indeed."

"If you're interested, I'll show you the list of groups that I'm going to call together."

He handed me a typed sheet listing:

the polysystematizers

the phenomenophile co-materialists

the dialectical telepathicians

the unreformed piatiletkian fellow-travelers

the revisionist anthroposophists

the discordant anthroposophists

the plurivalent dysharmonists

the contraceptual Yugoslavs

the paralyrical mediumists

the unresolved pro-ultra-red fanatics

the incubophile spiritualists

the unadulterated asymmetric revolutionaries

the intolerant polypsychists

the pro-Mussolinian anti-fascist terrorists of the extreme left

the contracop fruitarians

the uncoordinated metaphychists

the disseminated pararchists

the league for barbiturates

the committee for promoting psychoanalysis by correspondence

the Edouard Salton group

the dissident socio-Buddhists (aforementioned)

the non-active nihilating phenomenologists

the association of revolutionary anti-intellectuals

the revolting integral nullifiers

the initiated anti-Masonic trade unionists

and thirty-one Belgian groups.

"You can keep that document," Anglarès told me. "Do you have any objection to any of these groups?"

"None," I said.

85

"Good. And now I'm going to lunch."

He rubbed his hands together, saw a taxi and ran after it. He was in a good mood.

"It's funny that it should put him in a good mood," I thought, looking down at the hodgepodge again. "He doesn't take three-quarters of these people seriously himself"—as I now knew. The more I thought about it, the stranger I found his intense involvement in that sort of activity: meetings, more meetings, agitating, demonstrating, congratulating, protesting, altercating, breaking up. In the end I decided that if that's what kept him happy, he was free to do it; after all, it didn't bother me. Refusing to let this trouble me any longer, I got up and went on my way: I strolled over to my uncle's to get some money. As I wasn't supposed to be there until four o'clock, I didn't hurry. I wandered along the boulevards, my head quite empty, empty even of dreams. But, in the vicinity of Saint-Augustin, it occurred to me that the first time I met Odile it was in this part of the world. Then I remembered the silly pun that had marked my first meeting with Anglarès. Indeed, it was when I was coming away from my uncle's that I had met Odile for the first time: it must have been a little over 430 days ago, most likely 433. "A prime number," I said to myself, and that's when such a fantastic idea came to my mind that I stopped dead in my tracks. Then having thought about it further, I set off at a run. I felt like jumping over the benches but I didn't dare to. I didn't know how to hide my extreme state of excitement. I burst out laughing several times: it was most embarrassing. I couldn't go and see my uncle in that state. So I forced myself to do some complicated calculations in my head, and by the time I entered the Indo-Chinese lounge I was merely very cheerful. I thought that luck was on my side, as my uncle seemed to be in a good mood. In fact, everyone seemed to be in a good mood today. The day was getting better as it went along.

"What's new then?" he asked me with great cordiality.

He had grown ten times fonder of me since I had nearly, if not besmirched, then at least compromised, the family name.

"What's new? Well, I'm going to get married."

"Really. Do you have a woman in mind?"

"Of course I do," I replied, offended.

"Do you love her?"

"Of course."

I hid the main part of my idea which was that we would get married only in order to rescue Odile but that it would not commit us in any other way: I had thought of a way of helping her and of proving my friendship to her, only friendship, nothing more than friendship. It seemed such a perfectly pleasing solution, and I found it so ingenious that I was not even abashed by the length of time it had taken me to think of it.

"And what is your fiancée," asked my uncle, "called?"

"Mademoiselle Clarion."

"From a good family?"

"Excellent."

He made a face: it wasn't so much fun if I made a good marriage. I told him the story of Odile's life, more or less. He liked that better.

"I see, I see. Birds of a feather."

"You can call it that if you like. I'm going to go and fetch her."

"And you'll elope."

"And then we'll get married."

"Her family will object."

"We won't pay any attention to them."

"Do you think that's possible?"

I had no idea. He explained to me about weddings and what you had to do to get married. I was especially tickled by the idea of the three marriage banns and my uncle was even more so, thinking of the reaction of some members of the family.

"It's all set then."

What an organizer!

"What are you going to live on?"

That was my cue.

"Perhaps you could help us," I replied.

He started to laugh.

"Do you really think so?"

"Of course. You'd only need to give us twice as much as you're giving me."

"You're not shy about asking!"

"And I'll work. I'll give some lessons, for instance."

"I can't believe it. Has love made a changed man of you?"

I chose not to answer such a stupid question.

My uncle was a charming man, and what wouldn't he have done to play a good trick on the rest of my family? I came away with several thousand-franc notes in my pocket. I was pretty pleased with myself and I thought how wonderful one felt on a cold December day even when one had on a lousy overcoat with threadbare sleeves and a greasy collar. It occurred to me that I should buy myself a proper overcoat with the thousand-franc notes but I indignantly rejected the idea of such a fruitless waste of money that had been designated for a more worthy purpose. Meanwhile, I had to consult a railway time-table. In spite of my threadbare sleeves and greasy collar, I went into a very luxurious bar and ordered a port-flip as I had seen Saxel do. The timetable board reminded me that there was a train at 10:48: the one Odile had taken. There wasn't an earlier one and even if there had been another, I would have taken that one. 10:48 at night, so I was going to spend a twentieth of that day in a train. Pleased with this observation, I gulped down my beaten egg and took a taxi back to the hotel.

I packed my suitcase and went downstairs.

"Are you leaving, Monsieur Travy?" asked the manageress.

"Only for two or three days."

"Should we keep your room for you?"

"I've left all my things there."

I felt up to taking on all the landladies in the world, even the easygoing ones. A taxi took me to the Gare de Lyon; I put my suitcase in a locker. I now had about four hours to kill. I didn't want to go to the Place de la République: I wasn't in the mood. I phoned Vincent: not at home. So I had dinner, then waited patiently. It seemed an age, but when the time came for the passenger cars to be attached I was still feeling just as happy and I slept so well that I missed my station. I had to wait a long time before I could get back again. Then I took a bus to my final destination, which was a very small town. I had no reason to offer for coming to such a tiny town on such a cold December day. The first person I accosted in the street would have told me so. I went and left my bag at the hotel. They were very curious about me and I had no explanation ready. When I said nothing, they became even more curious and eyed me with definite suspicion. I didn't worry about that; I had a leisurely lunch. Then I went out. Some distance from the hotel, I asked the way. At the edge of the town, the Clarion family had a large house with a large garden, all very ordinary and surrounded by high walls. It was on the main road. I stopped in front of the gate: on the other side of it a dog came and howled. Passing locals watched me watching. I walked further. I took a path which skirted one of the walls but this wall was just as high as the others: and the path was a dead end. I turned back and found myself on the main road again face-to-face with suspicious natives. Everything seemed to be very complicated all of a sudden: beyond me perhaps. I wanted things to happen simply and without the love-story element: but how to achieve that? My courage failed me.

Some way away, and on the other side of the road, there was a clump of trees in the corner of a field. I went and sat down out of the wind and stared at the gate, in the hope that she might come out; a vain hope and somewhat cowardly wishful thinking. I stayed there about an hour, oblivious of the locals' curiosity, my feet frozen and my hands numb. A very sharp wind started to blow; I persisted with my watch but I began to sneeze. It must have been a bout of sneezing that made me look up, and over there between the trees I saw a window being closed. I felt sure now that she was going to come out; I got up and went down from my mound.

"Cold day for a walk," said a passing peasant.

"No, it's beautiful," I replied bravely and set off in the direction of the country.

When I'd gone two or three hundred meters and sneezed about ten times, I decided that it was time to retrace my steps. And then I saw Odile walking towards me. I didn't hurry and I was wondering to myself whether I should speak to her here, on the road, near her house. But when I got near her, she held out her hand.

"Roland, what are you doing here?" she said with a peal of laughter.

I didn't understand her bewilderment.

"I came to see you," I replied solemnly. She stopped laughing immediately and took my hand:

"Did you think of me?"

"Of course," I replied, "I did."

We had stopped in the middle of the road and I could feel the wind tearing my ears to shreds. I gave three loud sneezes. A car made us go up onto the shoulder.

"Poor old you," said Odile, "you've caught a terrible cold. Whatever made you go and sit over there?"

"I didn't want to arouse any suspicions. I'm taking you back with me."

She didn't laugh.

"I'm taking you back with me: if you want, that is. Because, wait till I explain. I got this idea yesterday in the Place Saint-

Augustin. This is it: we get married and share the money that my uncle'll give me if I get married. That way you won't need to live here any longer and you can do what you like. At least, as much as I can. Of course when I say we'll get married, I mean we'll go through the ceremony. Otherwise, we'll just stay good friends, won't we? That was my plan for getting you out of here. I've been wondering how I could get you out of here for ages. Then I thought of this. We'd share what my uncle gave us, you see, and we'd each live as we wanted. Still I hope we'd see each other as often as before, I hope."

I had to keep sniffing as I spoke. I stopped to give my nose a good blow.

"Of course," I went on, "if you don't . . ." I searched for a word . . . "like the idea, then I'll just have got myself a cold."

I said it with no hint of humor because it was a bad cold and I was shivering. I waited for her reply without daring to look at her.

She said to me: "What am I supposed to do in Paris?"

"I don't know."

"It's all the same to me if I'm here or there."

"I know."

A truck went by, making such a noise that we couldn't hear ourselves speak. It stopped outside one of the first houses on the edge of town.

"Would you like it if I said yes?"

The truck went off again pounding the paving-stones.

I nodded.

So she said: "We'll leave this evening."

I spent the rest of the day in a café watching people play billiards. I had dinner. I got the bus back to the station. It was an icy-cold December evening; I was drowsy with rum and aspirin. Two or three other people were waiting like me for a very local train that finally turned up. I went to sleep in my compartment. An hour later, I was at the buffet on Dijon station, sipping a hot toddy. Traveling is waiting: it was nearly 2:00 A.M. when Odile came in. She had a young man with her who was carrying her suitcase. As he stayed at a respectful distance, she gestured in my direction and said to him:

"That is Monsieur Travy."

He came forward and shook my hand.

"This is Gérard," she said.

The three of us sat down.

"Everything go all right?" I asked rather unconvincingly.

And everything had gone all right from packing to the slow night ride in the farmer's old van. His son listened as she spoke, calmly drinking a steaming black coffee. As for me, I felt I was coming down with a real fever. The Paris train was announced: once more we were out in the night pinched by the cold with the wind whistling up the long platforms. The young man was still carrying Odile's suitcase; we didn't speak. I was swaying. At the appointed time a splendid express came to a halt. Odile got in. Then I got in. I took Odile's case and went to look for seats. When I'd found two, I reserved them and went back to the door. Odile had got out again and was talking to Gérard. I looked somewhere else. There was a jolt as they attached the new engine, the seven minutes' stop came to an end, Odile got back in. Gérard stayed on the platform showing no signs of emotion. I held out my hand to him and said, "Thanks," and tried to pronounce a sentence. But the carriage door was shut and the train left. He waved his hand. In the compartment there were only two other people, who barely opened their eyes to look at us. They went straight back to sleep. Only the night-light stayed on. Odile leant over to me.

"How are you feeling?"

"Lousy."

She took my hand.

"You've got a temperature."

"It'll go: I had some aspirin and four hot toddies at the buffet

92

while I was waiting for you."

"Do you need anything?"

"No thanks. What about you, are you OK?"

"I'm OK."

She smiled, then let my hand go. I closed my eyes and didn't wake up again until Paris. I got Odile a room not far from mine and went home to bed: it was Odile who looked after me. I lost the thread of things more than once, and in my delirium I saw figures and these figures took the shape of numbers which had hostile, evil properties. They coagulated, dissolved, got transformed and degraded just like common living things or chemicals. They danced about frantically and I did not intervene at all in the patterns they were weaving. Beside me Odile read, or for hours on end watched the servants and the kitchen boys busying about in the courtyard. My head was full of the commotion in the kitchen, and sometimes two fractions banged into each other with a clatter of saucepans. When Odile went at night, when I thought I was sleeping, I turned over and over in my mind this sentence: there must have been something between that Gérard and Odile but it was none of my business. When she came back in the morning, the figures would begin their wild gyrations, playing their "delusions of genius" trick on me. A few days later something else bothered me: the police invaded the scene. They turned into numbers, added and multiplied, pouring out of every corner. I forced Odile to take totally unreasonable precautions, and in my desperate attempts to escape from that unruly mob I devised a thousand and one schemes which moved through the alluring landscapes of combinational topology and ended up relentlessly in total disaster. In the end, one day I made up my mind that I had better get myself out of this mess.

I found out that during the fortnight not a single policeman had put in an appearance, and none put in an appearance thereafter; better still, our families had no objection to our getting married, preferring to hear as little about us as pos-sible. So as soon as I was better, I started to fill out all the forms. I do believe that it was my first civic act. It wasn't great fun, but however much of a pain these things were they still had to be done: I had to accept their existence. I started the search for witnesses, one for Odile and one for me; I thought that Vincent and Saxel might deign to play this role. I went to see the former but he'd moved without leaving an address, so I tried to get in touch with the latter. He was now writing a miscellaneous column for *L'Humanité*. I waited an hour for him. He came at last; I was surprised that he seemed surprised to see me; he hesitated a moment before shaking hands. Feeling a bit awkward, I explained that I had come to ask him a favor: some-thing that might be a bit of a nuisance.

"I'd be delighted," he said very suspiciously.

He was looking at me with distinct hostility. I didn't dare continue.

"Oh well, it's not worth it," I said, "so long."

He called me back.

"I'm sorry if I'm a bit on edge. You see, since you signed that declaration, I find it a bit strange for you to come and see me."

This could only make sense in the context of some inter-group politicking. I realized that we couldn't avoid "having it out"; these people loved to "have things out"; stab each other in the back and then talk about it. Perhaps Saxel was con-tinuing the tradition. To me it seemed a futile sport. But in the circumstances I could not avoid taking up the bait:

"Listen, Saxel, I don't understand what you're talking about."

"Really?"

Then he took out of his wallet a small piece of paper and handed it to me: it was written in a tone of violent grandilo-quence. No one who read it could have doubted that Saxel was a traitor, a defector, an intriguer, a mischief maker. It went all through the story of the "spirit of Lenin," as well as two or three very unpleasant anecdotes about Saxel's private life, as it is called in polite circles. At the bottom of this scurrilous document I saw my signature.

"I might have known," I said, "I never signed that."

"You didn't?"

"I haven't been out for a fortnight: I've been ill and I haven't seen Anglarès for three weeks."

"I believe you but it's rather disturbing."

"Especially for me when I had nothing to do with it."

"I knew you wouldn't have signed a rotten thing like this."

"You think it commits me?"

"I'm afraid it does."

"Listen, Saxel, I don't want to take any more of your time. I'll be going."

"Didn't you want to ask me something?"

"It was nothing. Bye."

"Good-bye."

We shook hands and I left. As I went out, all sorts of expressions flashed through my mind, like "things are going from bad to worse" or "it's silly for a friendship to end like that" or "what a bizarre story." It seemed odd to lose a friend like that. I went into a café and phoned Anglarès. He wasn't at home. OK, I'd have to go to the Place de la République to find Vincent or get his address; some other pamphlet might have been written against him. I telephoned Odile as well to tell her about it; but she had gone out.

It was dark now but it was still too early to find Anglarès and his friends. I went home and waited in the dark until it was time. When I went out again after having had a chance to think about it, I felt quite cheerful. I got to the Place de la République about seven o'clock; there was quite a large group surrounding Anglarès. Vachol, Vladislav, and Chènevis were there, as well as others that I knew a little and others that I didn't know at all.

"We haven't seen you for a long time," said Anglarès, greeting me courteously.

"I've been ill."

"Nothing serious?"

"You can see for yourself."

The conversation took up from where I had interrupted it. Vladislav the painter was putting forward an ultra-leftist point of view and Chènevis was opposing it with an equally ultra-leftist point of view: they were having a big argument. I listened to them for a moment but, not being in the least interested in their intense polemics, I asked Anglarès for Vincent N.'s new address, for I was in fact curious to learn what had happened to him; he was still one of "ours" because I was given his address immediately. I went on:

"And the realignment that you had under way?"

Anglarès smiled: "There hasn't been any real realignment," he said, "but we've had excellent results."

He added in a low voice: "Salton's group has disbanded: that's why Vladislav has come over to us."

Just then the aforementioned declared: "We must bring about the Revolution by the most radically infrapsychic means and fight the bourgeoisie with what disgusts it most: excrement."

"We have to wallow in dirt and inhale the odor of crime," declared one of the neophytes.

"And in our fight let us not forget that mighty weapon: dementia praecox," said a little fellow who was hunched up like a chrysalis, or a good imitation of one. Anglarès told me that it was V., a former "integral nullifier."

"There will never be a Revolution unless we can find a technique for getting the entire bourgeoisie under our spell," said someone who looked very different.

"That's W.," Vachol whispered to me, "he's one of the 'incubophile spiritualists.' "

I realized that Anglarès's maneuvering had brought in disciples from more or less everywhere; I say "disciples," although for the time being they were still pretending to have their own ideas. As Anglarès seemed inclined to chat, I announced to him, discreetly, that I was going to get married. He started. Vachol, who had heard, frowned.

"You're getting married?" said Anglarès very scornfully.

I refrained from explaining my reasons. But: "Saxel is going to be a witness," I said.

He grabbed his pince-nez and put it astride his nose. He gave me a searching look; he had made undeniable progress in magnetism.

"You're pulling my leg, Travy."

He had a beautiful voice: deep, subtle, rich.

"Why on earth should I be?" I said.

He didn't answer, and settled himself into his pose. Vachol cut in: "He doesn't know what's been happening."

"Happening?" I asked.

"What," someone exclaimed, "you don't know what's been happening?"

"No, what?"

Chènevis decided it was his turn to pipe up: "Saxel's a bastard: we've thrown him out!"

"He ought to see our tract," said Vachol. Someone handed it to me. I reread it carefully: there was nothing actually false in it but it was all misleadingly expressed.

"Well, what do you know, my name is there," I commented.

"You're a member of our group, aren't you?" Vachol retorted.

"What's your objection?" asked Chènevis.

They didn't seem pleased that I expressed surprise at seeing my name at the bottom of something that I hadn't read.

"You may still be harboring some friendly feelings for Saxel," said Anglarès, "but you must understand that ethics come before friendship. Stick to our principles we must, stick to our principles we do."

His acolytes were silent, overawed by this self-praise. Anglarès himself made his hair ripple gently by an adroit shake of the head and directed his penetrating gaze at a carafe of tap water. "Ugh," I thought to myself. It seemed pointless even to tell him that it was not a question of choice as far as I was concerned, so I let him wallow gloriously in his error. I put a few francs in the saucer and got up. Why cast pearls before swine? I left without saying another word. I was not sorry to have experienced this little incident: so these were the great "free" minds?

What about Vincent? How would I be received by him? Had he put his name on the bottom of the excommunication order? I couldn't remember. If he hadn't signed, how could Anglarès have mentioned him so calmly? I went into a news-agent's and wrote a postcard, arranging to meet with him the next day: he turned up.

"So you're better?"

"How did you know?"

"I came to your hotel twice; they told me you had a bad bout of flu. I was going to drop you a line today or tomorrow. What's new?"

I replied out of habit: "Nothing much."

I went on: "I mean: I shan't be seeing Saxel again and I'm not going to the Place de la République anymore."

"Understood."

"You know what's been happening?"

"I can guess. Saxel saw your name and he got mad. You saw your name and you got mad."

"Precisely."

"It's a common trick. I've seen it happen dozens of times."

"What about you, did you sign the thing against Saxel?"

"Same as you. But it won't happen to me again. I'm tired of

the whole thing, tired and exhausted."

"Anyway, I didn't come to talk about all that but to ask if you could do me a favor, something that's a bit of a drag."

"What's that?"

"To be a witness at my wedding."

"It's a drag or it's a joke?"

"No, no, I'm not joking: it's something extremely simple."

"Really, you're getting married?"

"Does it seem so odd to you?"

"Frankly, yes. In any case, you can count on me."

I was on the point of giving an explanation for this wedding that he found so surprising, but I decided against it, not wanting to sound as if I was apologetic about doing something so peculiar. Setting aside the scorn in which we held bourgeois conventions and the bureaucratic rituals of a capitalist regime, 'I wondered to myself what sort of a person I must seem, if the possibility of my getting married seemed so unlikely, even to the only person who knew me a little. I could feel the mask behind which I was hiding, the disguise that I was wearing, fading or falling off bit by bit but the shreds that were left still made up the facade that I had believed to be me and which I thought I had adopted for life, that of a weakling, weighed down by misfortune.

"You're not listening to what I'm saying," observed Vincent.

"Oh, pardon me."

He gave me an understanding look which until recently would have greatly annoyed me: he obviously thought I was in love.

"What were you saying about all these people?"

"I was saying that the root cause of all their mistakes is their crude dialectic; they always aim at the lowest common denominator, and one can see why. There are two ways of lacking a particular attribute: because you're incapable of it or because you don't aspire to it, because it's beyond you or beneath you.

"What do you mean?"

"Well, childhood can be put forward as an 'ideal' state for mankind as long as it's taken as the highest aim, and it isn't just that one can't do any better, because all the potential of childhood has been developed rather than because of an inability to grow up. These people who preach the virtues of childhood dredge around for them in the basement of the unconscious, in the junk room, on the scrap heap; so they only manage a caricature. Just look at what their pseudo activity is made up of. They behave like 'big children' with all the connotations that has of being mentally retarded. Look at all these conferences, manifestos, exclusions! They're just childish games! They play at being seers, revolutionaries, wise men; it's a farce! Look at their experiments, their doctrines, their pretentiousness, their self-importance; it's all puerile, puerile!"

"So you've grown up?"

"That's right. Take another example: inspiration. They see inspiration as the opposite of artistic technique and they aim to have a constant supply of inspiration by rejecting technique, even the technique that gives meaning to words. So what do we get? Inspiration vanishes: you can hardly use the word inspiration for people who roll off strings of metaphors and reel off puns by the yard. They lurk in the dark hoping to unearth the hammers and sickles that will break the chains and sever the links that bind man. But they've lost their own freedom. They've become slaves to twitches and mechanical reactions and they congratulate themselves on being turned into typewriters; they even set themselves up as an example, which shows what naive demagogues they are. They think the future of the mind lies in their prattle and their stutterings! Quite the opposite, I don't believe that a true poet is ever 'inspired': both the lowest and the highest denominator are beneath him, he's above technique and inspiration, which come to the same thing as far as he's concerned, because he's in full possession

of both of them. The really inspired person is never inspired:
he's always inspired: he doesn't go looking for inspiration and
he doesn't get up in arms about artistic technique."

No doubt the Arab that I'd seen one day on the road from
Bou Jeloud to Bab Fetouh which skirted the walls of the town
was just such a poet. It had been raining but the sun was drying
the mud on the road. In the last puddles of water I could see
the last clouds drifting away. There was no reason for me to do
so, but I attributed a multiplicity of meanings to this image.
Vincent looked at me.

"You're very engrossed today."

"It's because you're giving me food for thought."

"And what do you think?"

"That I'll have to find another witness because Saxel doesn't
want to do it."

"Will that be so difficult?"

"I don't know anyone in Paris except an uncle who'd refuse,
even though he is well disposed towards me."

"And your," he hesitated, "... fiancée ... ," he gave an
embarrassed smile, "doesn't know anyone either?"

"No, I'll have to pay someone to stand in."

"You make me think of an American comedy with your hunt
for witnesses."

"All these complicated social conventions are a bit beyond
me. It's true that there's a difference between thinking that
something you can do is beneath you, and despising what you
can't do. There must be a proverb about it?"

"I'm afraid there must."

"You're not afraid of proverbs, are you?"

"A little, now I've got used to everything being topsy-turvy."

"I'll have to think about what you said."

"Do you want me to ask one of my friends to be a witness?"

I said "yes," thanked him solemnly and left him thinking. The
next day or the same day I found a very interesting letter from

Anglarès in my box:

"My very dear friend . . . provided that . . . I'll take care not to . . . one might wonder if . . . I don't know if there are grounds for . . . in any case . . ."

I commented: "Look at that, same style as the magistrate," and threw his missive in the wastebasket.

The wedding took place at the beginning of March. Vincent was there, naturally, and his friend Texier and my uncle. We didn't like to refuse his offer of a drink. He told us anecdotes about Indochina until midday; then he left. Texier asked where we were going to have a meal. I made a face:

"A wedding breakfast!"

"It won't be the first time the four of us have had a meal together," said Vincent.

"That's true."

I was aware of being in an extremely bad temper. I did my best not to make any further show of such regrettable feelings. Odile was smiling, her thoughts far away. I named a restaurant: everyone agreed. Texier wanted to pay for the taxi, and another round of drinks. He insisted on our selecting expensive oysters and rare wines, and everything he said and did was designed to turn this into a celebration, though among close friends. He drank a lot and talked as much. He reminded me of Saxel, but stripped of his doctrinal layer. I listened to him with deliberation and noticed that Odile's thoughts really seemed far away. As for Vincent, he seemed curious, but about what? I began to think that I had been really stupid not to explain to them the reasons for the wedding. I could hardly confide in them over the dessert. So all I could do was listen to Texier, look at Odile and allow myself to be scrutinized by Vincent. We all liked a laugh, so the lunch was quite lively. It was over three hours later when we left the restaurant, and I was worried that Texier would suggest going for a walk or to the cinema. He suddenly remembered an urgent appointment and left us. Vincent had work to do; he went with Texier. They ran to catch a bus.

"So, Odile, it wasn't too bad?"

"Of course not."

"Are you sure?"

"Sure."

"OK. Let's take a short walk?"

"Good idea."

She took my arm. We went down Rue Washington.

"Do you want to come with me as far as La Muette?"

"What on earth are you going to do in that part of Paris?"

"I'm going to give a lesson."

"You're incredible."

"Why's that? Because I give lessons? I only started a week ago. Texier got them for me: very well paid, you know. It'll bring us in a little extra, won't it?"

"I suppose so."

"Are you cross?"

"Why didn't you tell me about it?"

"I don't know. There's something else I haven't told you."

She didn't answer.

"I've made a discovery."

"What is it?"

"A negative discovery, unfortunately."

I thought she faltered, but it was in my imagination. She looked up at me, very serious.

"My life is even more of a mess than I thought it was."

She looked as if she couldn't believe her ears.

"For years I've been mistaken about myself and I've lived under a misapprehension. I used to think I was a mathematician. Just recently I've realized that I'm not even an amateur mathematician. I'm nothing at all. I don't know anything about it. I don't understand anything about it. It's terrible but that's how it is. And do you know what I was capable of doing? Do

103

you know what I used to do? Calculation after calculation out of sight, out of breath, aimless, purposeless and totally absurd. More often than not I got drunk on figures; they pranced in front of me until my head was swimming until I was dazed. And I thought that's what math was about. For years I've been turning myself into a moron doing research without an end, a beginning, or even a middle. Imagine a calculating machine going berserk. That's me, that was me. It's unbelievable, isn't it?"

She certainly didn't believe it. Without opening her mouth, I heard her shout: "But you're quite crazy!"

"I was. Or rather I was childish. I was pretending to be a mathematician. I thought sand castles were algebraic constructions and puzzles were geometric theorems. And my sand castles crumbled and my puzzles got all muddled up without a figure taking shape. As for my ideas about math, first of all I can't take credit for them, and secondly I think they're ruined by fashionable theories which have nothing to do with the true nature of that science. Anyway, it doesn't matter much. The main thing is: I'm not at all what I thought I was. It's a bit disturbing, you see, because I was happy in a kind of way kidding myself like that. It's Vincent who brought it home to me, without meaning to. I realized that what he criticized in the others was true of me too. I looked at the beam in my own eye. I had built myself a hut with the leftover bits and pieces of my ambition; I've got to move out now, it's been blown down. I've no refuge now, I never had one. The truth is harsh. So now I'm giving lessons: Latin lessons."

But Odile didn't believe me. I left her at the Arc de Triomphe where I got the bus. I met her again to go and have dinner at my old uncle's; we spent the evening listening to him playing the accordion, with the rings on his fingers shining. At midnight he saw us out. We got a taxi home; we didn't say much: an occasional remark about our benefactor. When I was back in my room all alone, I felt so bereft of hope that I started to cry, like a child.

So, there I was, married. This was not to change my life in any way and yet, one day, all of a sudden, jolting around in a shapeless daydream on a bus, it occurred to me how amazingly well the change of civil status coincided with the change in my life, a change that had taken place without my being really aware of it, as always: quite simply I had become very unhappy. I marveled now at the state of blissful torpor in which I had lived before: just a few weeks before. I had been proud of my misery then and lacked no petty sources of satisfaction. When the illusion faded, it was an end of the vain conceit. The hours that I used to spend lost in the soft cocooning darkness of capital sigmas and various indices had got taken up by my teaching duties and the long journeys across Paris that they involved. It was rare of me to find time to be alone with Odile; if we ate together in the evening, it was with friends, new friends, sometimes even new friends of our new friends. One of them persuaded her to "do something in films." I urged her to accept. Sometimes I would go and fetch her out at the Billancourt studios, but then I met all sorts of people I didn't want to see. I advised her to move, it was a long way from Billancourt to the Port Saint-Martin. By now we were only having dinner together two or three times a week, but I knew very well that fate was not to blame for this unhappy state of affairs. I was not losing a friend: I was distancing myself from her, I was distancing myself from myself. But why did Odile allow herself to be dragged along by my ill will? Why didn't she take a stand against the tide of events, against the way in which I wanted and at the same time did not want to warp the shape of her life? And how was it possible for her not to realize that this distancing was all my doing? I was digging a trench full of well-marked booby traps. It was enough to make you laugh: a trench with booby traps. I wasn't proud of my first attempts at metaphor. It was enough to make you laugh, but was it really funny? Why this need to make faces? I hated clowns and perhaps myself too.

The bus passed a shadowy figure who was strolling along. I got up as soon as I recognized him. I got off the moving bus and ran after him. Vincent was out for a walk; I wanted to have a serious talk with him. I waited for the ritual greetings to be over, then I came straight to the point.

"Don't you think Texier's fallen for Odile?"

"What makes you think that?"

"I don't think, I know. Vincent, I must explain something to you: Odile and I are only good friends, do you understand?"

"I understand."

He didn't seem surprised. I went on:

"We got married for reasons of convenience, it'd take too long to tell you all about it, but you do understand, don't you? That's why I asked you the question."

"What are you getting at?"

"Don't you think I should speak to Texier?"

"And what would you say to him?"

"Of course I'd feel a little stupid. But still!"

"Still what?"

"I don't know, I don't know anymore. You think I'm crazy, don't you?"

"Do you mind if I ask you a few questions?"

"Go on."

"They're rather personal, but it's you who brought it up."

"Go on."

"I'm very fond of you, you know, Travy."

"Thanks, me too."

"Why don't you ever want to show your feelings?"

"Is that your first question?"

"No."

Vincent went on: "Don't you know people find it strange that you and Odile live a few miles apart?"

"I don't know anything at all. I don't care what other people think and anyway why should it mean anything that we don't live in the same place?"

"That's what you say."

"What's your next question?"

"Why don't you love Odile?"

"You make me laugh: it's not a question of why. I don't love her, that's all, you can't give a reason."

"Maybe you should speak in the past tense?"

"I'd never have believed that you'd use such unsubtle psychology! How crafty! They've been friendly for over a year now, so they must want to go to bed together. That's really something! A friendship that turns into love, a good story for a novel: for a silly novel like all novels are. I abominate psychology, especially that sort of psychology, everyman's psychology, idiot's psychology."

He gave a little bow.

"So you see I'll never love that woman, never never never because I don't want to prove the idiots right. And even if I did love her, I wouldn't show it, because of that."

"That's just what's happening."

"I was waiting for you to say that. It was obvious. I'm telling you, Vincent, I'll always resist clichés like that. Do you think it's always the most banal thing that happens?"

"Of course loving a woman is the most banal thing that can happen."

"That's not what I mean."

"What do you mean?"

"I don't know. What I mean is that you're wrong about me because of your lousy psychology, of your stupid science."

"But it's not a matter of psychology or of science, Travy! It's a matter of you getting to know yourself and not acting like a child."

"You're so sensible!"

"Travy, why do you insist on making yourself unhappy?"

"And why do you insist on my loving Odile?"

"Because you do love her."

"You're wrong. If I loved her, how do you think I could fool myself to the extent of thinking I didn't love her?"

"You don't think you can fool yourself to that extent?"

"No."

"Have you never fooled yourself to that extent?"

"You're getting pretty near the bone!"

He saw my face and said, "I'm sorry."

"No, no, don't be sorry, go on!"

"I'm sorry to have said what I did. I've no right to. How will you be able to forget what I've said now?"

"I've got a very bad memory."

We walked on in silence for a while.

"Haven't you anything else to ask me?" I said then.

He smiled.

"It's ridiculous and pretentious of me to try to give you advice, don't you think?"

"Oh," I replied, "you haven't given me any advice and anyway, as you said, I brought the subject up. In any case I'm sorry about some of the things I said."

We apologized mutually for a while longer and parted with a friendly handshake.

It was I who had provoked the "don't-you-love-her?" question, the question that I refused to formulate myself. I was scared of it and I had ended up hearing it with my own ears. I knew I didn't love her; I knew it but now I felt the need to assert it; and yet I was so certain about it that I even sometimes caught myself imagining what my love for Odile would be like, what it would be like to love someone. I always ended up being sure that I didn't; there was no need for me to imagine it, it was the truth: I didn't love the woman. I alternated between hating Vincent who had upset me so greatly and hating myself. The greatest agony was being in Odile's presence; all I could think about was her body and my obscene thoughts were in inverse proportion to the lofty heights that I wanted my friendship to scale. It was agony: I was so certain that I didn't love her! Now that I was deprived of the imaginary aim that I had set myself, and bereft of any interest in life or outside of it, I dwelt incessantly on my own unhappiness and loneliness. I lived out a mediocre existence not even alleviated as much as it might have been by alcohol, for I shuddered with disgust at the idea that people might have said knowingly of me as I vomited, "He's drowning his sorrows in drink." I avoided any sign of weakness that might have been justified by my feelings of despair and I managed to go about my business in such a way that nobody noticed that I was beginning to crack up. But in fact, the strain of it was driving me nearly mad.

Vincent had given up the attempt to bring me to self-knowledge; I knew he was wrong: that did not alter the sort of trust that I put in him. I felt him keeping an eye on me, which irritated me somewhat; I thought that I was capable of looking after myself and I braved the storm, teetering on the edge of a dark abyss. Early in the summer, when I had all my time on my hands, I felt as though there was a threatening void before me.

That was when Vincent turned up.

"What are you doing this summer?" he asked me.

"Nothing."

"Are you going away?"

"Why would I be going away?"

"I'm going to Greece."

"Oh, what a strange idea."

"It's not an idea, it just happened."

"What do you want to go and look at ruins for?"

"I'd like to go and have a look. Don't you like traveling?"

I hesitated.

"I was going to say 'I don't like anything' but that sounds a bit presumptuous."

"My parents used to travel a lot," I added, "and they took me with them; I can hardly remember anything about it. The only trip that has meant anything to me was with the army: there's a strange way to see the world."

"You were in Morocco?"

"Yes. Something there made a big impact on me; I mean, it affected me profoundly, something that I didn't understand, nothing more came of it, but it has lived on in me like a slow-burning candle that nothing could blow out. My life began over there. I was born with boots and my zouave's hat on my nut, haven't I ever told you about it? No? Well, I haven't told anyone, except Odile."

I stopped myself: "Why on earth am I talking so much?" But wasn't Vincent my friend just as Odile was? I remembered what she had said to me when I'd told her the secret of my birth, one day during our first winter. No doubt I shall die as I was born, but could that part of me ever die?

"Far away?" Vincent asked me.

He must have thought I was thinking about Odile, whereas I was just thinking about myself.

"It had been raining," I went on, "and I was floundering along the road. The winds were blowing the clouds away fast. There was a lone Arab gazing at what I was incapable of seeing. The sky was reflected in the water. That happened on the road from Bou Jeloud to Bab Fetouh which skirts the walls of the town. Do you know Morocco?"

"Yes, but not Greece."

"There are no ruins in Morocco except a few that the French have excavated, for their own enjoyment."

"I hope there aren't only ruins in Greece. Wouldn't you like to come with me and find out?"

"You think I should go to Greece?"

"I don't think you should: I'm inviting you to. I'm inviting you on Agrostis' behalf."

"Why is he inviting me?"

"Because he likes you, I expect. We'll go in his car, it'll be a wonderful journey right across Europe. We can stay with him for a fortnight at Glyphada. It's on the coast near Athens. After that he's going to join his parents in Egypt and we can do what we like. From what I hear, you don't need much money to live on. We can do a trip to the islands and then get back under our own steam. If you travel deck class, it doesn't cost much: and we'll be back in Marseilles. What do you say? Ask your uncle for a small advance. And don't forget that you'll be Agrostis' guest."

I couldn't see why that young man would want my company. I hardly knew him.

A week later I was waiting for Odile in a café to tell her I was going.

"What's up now?" she asked in an ironic, anxious voice.

"Nothing serious. I just wanted to say good-bye before I went. I'm going to Greece," I said importantly.

She said nothing for a minute, and then she said it must be a nice trip and she was sorry she couldn't come too.

"Can't you really?" I said, as though I'd asked her.

She looked at me, I turned my head and I could see that she was sad, not saddened: sad. I blushed.

"Why do we never see each other anymore?" she said.

I refrained from saying, "That's life." I wasn't quite stupid enough to say, "That's life." She placed her hand on mine and said "Why?" again. She had on gloves, which seemed strange to me. Her glove seemed to be appealing to me. I said: "I don't know."

Indeed I did not know what to say. I was sitting next to a woman: something warm and perfumed. I turned towards her and saw her crossed thighs under a close-fitting dress, then I looked up and my eyes met hers and they held the meaning of everything said between us.

"I think it's my fault," I stuttered, "I seem to have driven you away from me."

I had never realized that she could be so close to me.

"For months," I said, "we've hardly seen each other and yet . . ."

I stopped; hadn't I told Vincent? I didn't love her, I won't love her. If I had gone on in that vein, it would have turned into a love story: what a happy ending! So I asked her what plans she had for the summer. She told me she was going to the sea for her films. I congratulated her for getting on so well in her career and then told her how my trip had come about. Then I had nothing more to say to her.

But, after a pause, she said, "There's something terrible about you, Roland."

I didn't blanch or blush but I immediately thought I knew where the conversation was leading. I didn't want it to go anywhere. So I got an answer ready to dispel any hope when she said in a composed voice, "I love you, Roland."

It had happened: I didn't manage to stop it. I sniggered to myself. Then I weakened and asked myself, "Do I really not love her?" I was about to swallow my pride but she misunderstood my silence. She got up, held out her hand.

"Farewell," she said, "I hope you have a good holiday without thinking of me."

I gave a bow and murmured, "I shall think of you."

I do not think she heard; she paused a moment. Then her hand vanished.

I left for Athens the next day about midday. In fact that day we only got as far as Dijon.

Agrostis drove according to a well-known formula; he "made good time," then stopped frequently for a drink. We did not see any of the interesting sights between Paris and Greece but we got to know a lot of restaurants, cafés and bars in Switzerland, Austria, Hungary and Yugoslavia. We crossed flat countries and hilly countries with the same élan. Not very accustomed to alcohol, I was in a constant state of inebriation; I saw towns floating, trees dancing, mountains leaping. The only stable objects seemed to be bar counters. We weren't interested in central Europe as it whirled past us; after that, the road was full of surprises, the alphabet changed, the glasses smelt of piney resin, the drinks were cloudy white and the sky got deep blue. We were speeding down a sort of highway that had long ago been a sacred way. "Just you wait," said Agrostis, who was forgetting to be modishly and Parisianly disdainful now that we were getting close to Athens. We didn't have to wait long: a large town with a fortified castle rising up in the middle of it. We made straight for the outskirts, then at the end of a street full of shops we came to a large square covered with chairs; we ground to a halt. Agrostis took us over to a table and sat down; the idea of the game seemed to be to try to occupy the greatest number of chairs possible. Large glasses of water, mezes and small glasses of alcohol were placed in front of us; our shoes were cleaned, we bought pistachio nuts. Friends of Agrostis came and chatted with us; they were all poets, very courteous and up to date with what was being published in France. A discussion got under way and continued on the roof veranda of an inn, while we tucked into delicious local dishes. Then we went and had an ice cream on Constitution Square; then we drank whiskey in the garden of an open-air nightclub; and about four in the morning we went and had a late snack in a well-known dairy bar. Dawn was breaking when we got to the villa in Glyphada that Agrostis' parents were leaving for him while they went to Egypt.

We lived there free of charge, and no doubt perfectly "happy." At least that must have been true of Vincent, who always managed to live for the moment. I admired him for it but I was weighed down with a number of memories from which I could not free myself. I was tortured by the idea of happiness now: I was worried by how very real my weakness was and how truly mistaken I had been. Happiness eluded me because I had a real reason for feeling unhappy, and no longer simply because I was leading an existence that was impoverished, vacillating, handicapped by the unlucky dice I threw for myself. The worst thing was that I now had something in me that resembled a grain of hope, a grain which was not rotting now that I was far from Paris. So, although sometimes I was full of anguish, I gave the impression of being a carefree, witty soul.

It was only after more than a week that we got round to seeing the sights, our determination to be modern having been satisfied by this display of indifference. We climbed the Acropolis. We stopped on the way up. On the right a garden dotted here and there with ruins attracted our attention. Some children were playing. We stepped over broken columns, statues lying on the ground, and we reached the theater. Three or four modern Greeks were sitting on the tiered steps reading. I walked across the pit and sat down. I had never imagined that a marble seat could be so soft nor that stone could be so pliant and delicate; warmed by the sun, it almost felt like a human body. Vincent came and sat with me. We opened our eyes. This was a theater: the Theater. The mountains were a continuation of the stage, which was exactly level with the horizon: beyond it there was nothing but sky, a sky as unspoilt by the works of man as was the nature around it. Here there was no decline, no deterioration, no degradation. Before this harmony sending out its wide ripples, I was no longer aware of any limits or contradictions. It seemed as if next to me had come to sit the Arab I had met one day, somewhere towards the west, on the road from Bou Jeloud to Bab Fetouh.

My story ends here. After that I went on living: naturally; or rather I started to live; or should I say I started to live once more. So, I finally got up from the seat I was in and we continued our climb. A few days later, Agrostis took us to Delphi to see the eagles soaring over the sacred forests; then he left for Egypt and that same day we set off on a tour of the Cyclades. I decided to stop on one of these islands; I nearly stayed on Santorini, the most remote island, leaving it with reluctance. But Vincent dragged me away from its volcanic fumes and accompanied me as far as Paros. The fishing boat moved away, carrying him off towards the small ship; then the smoke moved behind the hills and I was alone again. I stayed in a hotel a little outside and above the village and right beside the sea; from the little terrace outside my room my main view, apart from the fishermen at work and at leisure, was of the movements of an old man: every morning he would go from the little town up to his windmill and chase away the birds that were hiding in the thatch roof, but the sails of his windmill did not turn more than once a week. Then he would sit down on a small bench and look straight ahead. From time to time he would knock on the thatch with a big stick and the birds would fly off chirping. In the evening he would go down to sleep in one of the little white-washed or blue-washed houses along the beach, which was strewn with fishing nets. When he noticed me dreaming on my terrace and later working away there recovering my lost feeling for numbers, he shifted his bench to have me in his field of vision. That way he kept me company.

I had one last block to overcome. I still couldn't act in all human simplicity. But I knew what was wrong and in my solitude I turned over in my mind the circumstances of my life one by one, finding everywhere signs of my own tendency to belittle myself, to do myself down, to suffer. I knew also where to find the last vestiges of this tendency: how could I not have known! The sheer strength of my obstinacy still filled me with anguish sometimes; it was a puerile and devilish obstinacy based now on the most slender of motives, or lack of motive, such as not wanting to be told "I-told-you-so." My false pride in refusing to live like everyone else was just childishness, because that was how I was living anyway and I loved her. I just, quite simply, loved Odile, as a man loves a woman, as he should love her. From the moment I recognized my love, it grew stronger and started to get the better of my self-consciousness, which I had now very nearly overcome.

About a month after my arrival in Paros I received two letters, one from Vincent giving me rather dismal news of our small Paris world; the other—well, I left it unopened. But I packed my bags and bade farewell to the old man from the windmill. At the poste restante in Athens I found a second letter that I left unopened as well. I sent a telegram to Vincent telling him that I was on my way home and I took the first boat bound for Marseilles. The shores of Cephalonia faded. I was taking back with me the promise of something meaningful: something begun on the island. I was going back to France, not so as to eke out an existence that I had emptied of all reality by willing misfortune upon myself, but so as to fight back and win, so as to reconquer what I thought I had lost: a woman's love. When I left Morocco I had seen the same skyline on the horizon but what could I understand then? Self-begotten unhappiness, puerile ingenuousness, my own pride that held me prisoner, my prolonged childhood that became a sort of old age and that's what I took for freedom. These fetters broken, these illusions dispersed, I no longer feared a relapse, I no longer feared being a "normal" person: from that starting point, I knew that I could attain greater things. To live in the world I had to live in was a hard task, much harder than chasing one's own tail, or balancing on a pinhead. And if it was great-ness I was after, I wouldn't find it in some pathological condition: the days of supercilious scoffing were over.

I no longer wanted to resist the love of another but to affirm my own. When we got to Marseilles, I didn't yet know that the battle was already won. I anxiously scanned all the objects that were piled up and spread out to make a port, and all the pieces of architecture out of which came diverse dins, the bustle and babel of which it seems life is constituted. The boat docked beside a customs shed. Behind a barricade of hustlers barking out hotel names and porters straining at the leash, I saw Odile waiting for me.

Notes

p. 3   The Rif Mountains are in northern Morocco. In the late nineteenth century Morocco was considered to be in the Spanish sphere of influence. The treaty of Fès (1912) made Morocco a French protectorate, while leaving certain areas, such as the north coast, to the Spanish, hence a later reference to Spanish Morocco. During the uprising of the Berber leader Abd el-Krim against the occupying French and Spanish forces, the Rif became an important battleground. "French" Morocco finally became independent in 1956.

p. 4   "Shleuhs": a Berber tribe from the Atlas Mountains. The word came to mean *foreigners,* and in World War II, *Germans.*

p. 4   Charles Martel (c. 688-741) was ruler of northern Gaul, and halted the advance of the Saracens at Poitiers in 732.

p. 4   Cid Campeador (c. 1043-1099): (El Cid) Spanish national hero who drove the Moors from Valencia in 1094.

p. 6   "spahis": North African cavalry corps.

p. 13   "the Party": the French Communist Party (P.C.F.) was founded in 1920, after a scission in the Section Française de l'Internationale Ouvrière (French Socialists).

p. 21   "Polytechnique": Ecole Polytechnique: exclusive tertiary institution for training military officers.

p. 22   "But I soon realized . . .": a reference to Nietzsche's strong attack on Christianity in *Der Antichrist* (1895). In Greek mythology the white horse (Pegasus) is the symbol of poetic inspiration.

p. 22   "Papusism": Papus was the pseudonym of Encausse (1865-1916), French doctor and occultist.

p. 24   "The flaccid crocodile . . .": "Le crocodile amorphe aux lèvres de corail / descend sans se presser la rue de Montmirail."

p. 25   "Manon": a reference to the early French novel, L'Abbé Prévost's *Manon Lescaut* (1731). This is both a love story and a portrait of society.

p. 25   "the cracodile cracks Odile": "Le crocodile croque Odile."

p. 40   Jaurès: Jean Jaurès (1859-1914), French socialist and pacifist who founded *L'Humanité* (familiarly referred to as *L'Huma*) as a Socialist newspaper. It became the organ of the Communist Party in 1920.

p. 50   "*Cahiers du bolchevisme*": theoretical journal of the Communist Party in the mid-1920s.

p. 66   Fermat: Pierre de Fermat (1601-1665), French mathematician, the first to conceive of differential calculus, and considered, along with Pascal, as the founder of probability theory.

p. 66   Brouwer: Luitzen Brouwer (1881-1966), Dutch topologist and logician, and founder of modern "intuitionism," which objects to the unrestricted use of Aristotelian logic (including the law of the excluded middle).

p. 74   Claude Bernard (1813-1878), pioneer of experimental physiology. Bernard, who had originally wanted a literary career, later turned to theoretical and philosophical writing, setting out his belief in the role of intuition as the necessary starting point for "creative" experimental research.

p. 74   Jean-Martin Charcot (1825-1893), French neurologist famous for his work on hysteria and on hypnotic therapy.

p. 75   ". . .it went to the dogs": in French, "tomber en quenouille" means to fall into female hands. Throughout his work Queneau makes sly puns on his own name. "Queneau" contains the Norman dialect words for "dog" and "oak," hence his early autobiographical poem entitled "Chêne et Chien" (1937).

p. 110   "zouave": French infantry corps that served in North Africa.